A Credit To Your Race

A CREDIT TO YOUR RACE

A
NOVEL
BY
TRUMAN
GREEN

ANVIL PRESS • VANCOUVER

Anvil Press Publishers Inc.
P.O. Box 3008, Main Post Office
Vancouver, B.C. V6B 3X5 Canada
www.anvilpress.com

Library and Archives Canada Cataloguing in Publication

Green, Truman, 1945-
    A credit to your race / Truman Green. -- 2nd ed.

ISBN 978-1-897535-86-8

    I. Title.

PS8563.R417C7 2011   C813'.54   C2011-906410-3

Cover design by Derek von Essen
Interior design by HeimatHouse
Cover photo courtesy of the author
Author photo by Mishelle Arenal

Represented in Canada by the Literary Press Group
Distributed by the University of Toronto Press

Publication of this work is made possible by the City of Vancouver's 125th Anniversary Grants Program, the Office of Vancouver's Poet Laureate Brad Cran, the Canada Council for the Arts, the Canada Book Fund, and the Province of British Columbia through the B.C. Arts Council (Innovations Project) and the Book Publishing Tax Credit.

Printed and bound in Canada.

To Karonne

Chapter 1

It's been almost a year since everything happened. I thought I'd be over it by now but it keeps coming back into my mind ruining all of my plans to be happy. At least Mary's okay—that's the main thing. I've still got that letter she wrote, which turned out to be the first and last letter I ever got from her. That still kind of hurts. I should probably chuck it but something keeps telling me to hang on to it.

I had this dream where me and Mary actually did get out of here and everything worked out great for us and the baby, and nobody even noticed that we were different colours. Just like it would naturally be if the world actually was a sane place, which, of course, it isn't. People just always have to believe things that aren't true—like coloured people shouldn't go out with white people and stuff like that—and try to convince you that you're ignorant or something if you don't get their point. I used to really like my teachers, for instance. Now I'm kind of thinking they're not so special. If somebody would have told me that I'd be pissed off at Coach Willard I'd have thought he was nuts. So anyway...life in Newton, BC is not really impressing me all that much. Like, if I happen to run into somebody who gave me advice about what I should have done about the baby, I just get right out of there right away, without even talking to them, unless I absolutely have to.

We've got this little house on five acres at 6635 Roebuck Road in Newton, which is in Surrey, BC. My dad bought it for us by working as a sleeping-car porter on the Canadian Pacific Railway. My mom and dad got divorced when I was only three years old, so I don't remember him much. I still like him, though, which kind of bugs my mother sometimes. After my dad went back to live in the States, sometimes I used to see my mom lying in the tall grass out behind the house, at the edge of the woods, crying. She'd always be trying to hide herself from Sarah and me, so I never let on that I'd seen her.

My mom waits on tables for her sister, Adele, who owns the Dixie Chicken Inn, which is this chicken and steak place where they sell illegal beer and whisky under the table. There's a rumour that my aunt pays somebody off because she doesn't have a liquor licence, but I don't know if it's true or not. It's at ten-eleven Seymour Street, right next to a gangster hangout called The Penthouse.

Except for me being the wrong colour, I guess I should probably admit that Newton is an okay place to live. When I was a little kid my mom and dad and Sarah and me lived in a little tarpaper shack on my aunt's forty-acre farm on the King George Highway at Hunt Road. Before that we were up at Webster's Corners in Maple Ridge in another tarpaper shack way back in the bush, down a plank road, off the Dewdney Trunk Highway, where there used to be black bears hanging around scaring everybody. When I was three there was a little bear in the blackberry bush, poking its nose up through an opening and scaring me so bad that I couldn't even yell for my mom to come down from the house and get me. Mom has always said that that's why we moved away from Webster's Corners; that some day a bear was going to get one of her babies and drag him (or her) off into the woods.

A lot of white people around here just see coloured people as a good excuse to laugh at somebody to make themselves feel more important. Like Ray Mack, whose dad, Old Ray Mack, owns the Newton General

Store at Newton Road and King George, insisting that little coloured kids should wear their names on their clothes because we all look the same. I never did figure out why anybody would think that. What a stupid thing to say! Another thing that bugs me is that in the movies all the Negroes are fools or idiots. There's this one guy in the movies called "Stepin Fetchit." All he seems to be there for is to be laughed at by white people for being scared of everything, and running so fast as to be able to catch up with trains when something scares him. Also, in the movies all the Negroes are servants or slaves or hired hands of one kind or another. Even Mark Twain gets into the act by calling coloured people "niggers" all the time and having Jim, Huckleberry Finn's friend, being so stupid that he thinks that he, himself, is rich because he is worth eight hundred dollars as a slave. That really pisses me off. And in *Gone With The Wind*, starring Clark Gable, all the coloured people are dummies and goofballs; there's not one intelligent, serious coloured person in the whole movie, except maybe Hattie McDaniel who got the Academy Award for playing (what else?) a personal servant to Scarlett O'Hara. My mom says the people who run Hollywood should be ashamed of themselves because they should know about prejudice, especially because a lot of them got out of Europe to get away from stuff like that.

It's not in our school books, but my grandfather says that millions of slaves were brought over from Africa in sort of like chicken cages in slave ships and sometimes thrown overboard to sharks if they got too sick to be worth good money in America, where Thomas Jefferson and guys like him in the seventeen hundreds said everybody is created equal, and deserves to be able to pursue happiness, and not be alienated from freedom. My grandfather says that he came to Canada because in the Indian Territories in Oklahoma they were lynching coloured people all over the place, and that the Americans had more guts than Dick Tracy for calling the United States "the land of the free and the home of the brave" in their big national song, which is too hard to sing anyway.

I love my mother. She's worked so hard for us. I think her whole life has been about doing things for me and Sarah. When we got our telephone a few years ago, my mother would call me up from the Dixie Inn and say that the Pacific Stage would be at Roebuck and Newton at such and such a time, and I'd run all the way down on the gravel road to meet her and help her carry all the things she had brought home for us. Like, for instance, giblets, which are chicken guts which she could get really cheap from the Dixie Inn's kitchen; and sometimes even books that customers had left behind—like one time we got a copy of *20,000*

Leagues Under The Sea, by Jules Verne, which she read to us for months, mostly in the winter, in the living room by the oil stove. Even now, I have no idea how she's done all this stuff and managed to make it to our school events and my Little League games and Sarah's softball games. When I'd zoom through the shortcut through the bush on my way home from Bose Road Elementary, I'd always be in a hurry to get home so I could find out if my mom had come home from Vancouver so that I could be happy again.

Chapter 2

I guess I really found out for sure what it means to be a coloured boy when Mary wouldn't show me what she was reading when I went over to talk about going square dancing last summer. Turning into her yard on my bike, I could see her sitting on the steps reading a newspaper. This was probably the first time I had ever seen her reading a newspaper so I knew that it was something pretty important—like a war or something.

"Hi, Mary. Whatcha readin'?" I said, coming up the walk to the steps.

She looked up and took off into the house without saying anything. I sat down and waited for her.

"Hey, Bill," she said, coming back out without the paper, "You wanna go square dancing tonight?"

"Yeah. You know we're going square dancing. We

planned it last week. What were you reading that you had to go hide when you saw me coming?"

"Oh, nothing." She sat down on the steps with her back to me and looked out over the green meadow surrounded by all those white fence posts.

"Come on, Mary. You can't fool me. There was something in that newspaper."

She got up and went into the house to bring me the paper.

"Here, read it yourself."

The headline read:

"GOVERNOR DEFIES U.S. MARSHALS"

There was a picture of a man standing in the doorway of a schoolhouse, sneering at three other men with armbands that displayed the words *U.S. Deputy Marshal.* Below that were two little coloured girls marching past soldiers with fixed bayonets.

I stared at the page for a long time, trying to figure out what I could say to her. It was a rotten feeling. We never talked about this crazy thing that was happening in the States. Actually, I was embarrassed to admit that lots of people hated Negroes—not just Mary's old man. I liked to pretend to her that he was just plain nuts and probably the only man in Canada who was so silly about racial things. But now with this whole front page dedicated to telling about other white people who were just as full of hatred as Mr. Baker...

14

well, I just didn't know what to say. Maybe Mary would want to know if these people might be right. Maybe coloured people shouldn't go out with white people. In fact, Mr. Baker had already made Mary wonder about it when she was telling him how smart I was in school and what a bunch of good things the principal had said about me when I got that merit award. Mr. Baker's answer to that was that if I was so smart how come I didn't know that coloured boys aren't supposed to go out with white girls?

Mary was still gazing at the field when I got up and rode my bicycle way up the road out of reach of her questioning eyes. I had to get away. The whole thing was making me embarrassed and upset. When I was out of sight I stopped and threw my bicycle down by the side of the road and sat down in a field where the tall grass hid me.

Chapter 3

I was absolutely positive that something was wrong with being coloured when Richard Bailey wanted to hear me laugh "like a nigger," like some guy he'd seen in a movie at the Surrey Drive-In Theatre on the King George Highway, and when Mary's father started talking about something called "miscegenation" and "coons," not even caring that she was just a kid and shouldn't have to listen to that kind of stuff.

One day out in the hayloft at the back of her place, Mary said she was really starting to hate her father. Apparently he didn't have anything against me personally, but he had seen it happen too many times when he was in the army overseas. Same old story, he'd told her. Too many coloured soldiers (or whatever he called them) got white girls pregnant and then refused to marry them. These Canadian men of colour (as my aunt likes to call us) just up and left thousands of poor little white girls knocked up all over the world.

"But Mary," I said, pulling the hay out of her hair, "there's only about one coloured soldier in the whole Canadian army. Surely he couldn't be responsible for all this."

"About one, eh. Very funny," she said, laughing and getting into a better mood. "He also says they're built different than white men."

"Different? What's *that* supposed to mean?"

"I'll never tell," she said, laughing, which was one of her favourite sayings at the time.

Mary's parents went vacationing down to Sandy, Oregon that summer, which was really great because at least for those few days I didn't have to sneak around with her. I just walked right up her front steps like a regular human being and asked the babysitter (my sister Sarah, who's one year older than me), if Mary was ready to go yet. Mary's little brother, Jimmy, wasn't even eight then, but he must have caught something from his dad (like an infection or something) because he didn't approve of her going out with me either—which was really strange because you can see prejudiced grown-ups acting like that, but who'd expect it from a seven- or eight-year-old kid?

Regardless of Jimmy thinking it was his sworn duty to report on everything that happened, those two weeks were probably the best of my entire life. Besides just feeling like a normal human being and not having to hide around corners like a burglar all the time, we did all kinds of things that normal people do without thinking anything about it. Like roller skating at the Cloverdale Roller Rink on Bose Road, and sitting in the bleachers watching curlers sweep their rocks so they'd move faster. Square dancing at Princess Margaret High School was the best though, because we thought it was so funny to listen to the country music and we'd smile at the lyrics and "do-si-do," as they say, and everything that went with it. That first Saturday we even managed to go out to Redwood Park on the Pacific Highway and hang out around that tree house where two brothers lived for years way back in the forties.

If it was dark when we got back (which it usually was), we'd come down Roebuck, and circle around the back along the creek so Sarah wouldn't see us, then go in the hay barn and climb the ladder up to the loft. A lot of the bales would be falling apart, but up near the front of the barn, just in front of the big hay doors where bales are pulled through on pullies, there were about ten solid ones. And that's where we'd always end up lying together watching the stars— even reciting poetry, like that one that goes: "Slowly, silently, now the moon..."

Mary's favourite song was "Born Too Late" and mine was "All In The Game," which I could sing pretty well—or so I thought, anyway. Which reminds me of that time I sang "Shop Around" to my mother, which made her cry.

If I try to figure out exactly how things got out of hand and we got carried away that last night before the Bakers got back, I'd have to probably chalk it up to being happy and sad all at the same time. There were lots of times when we'd be lying together and kissing with the stars coming through and everything—just generally making out—but knowing the same old stupid sneaking-around routine would be starting up soon put us in a kind of desperate mood. Anyway, whatever the reason, things didn't happen like they normally did, and where we'd always stop and go home, something happened that night and we ended up going a lot further than we'd intended.

Chapter 4

The Bakers got home the following Sunday just in time to take Mary and Jimmy to church. After the service, Mr. Baker took Mary up to talk to Reverend Phillips about her immorality. Don't get me wrong. It wasn't about anything in the barn. He wanted to show Mary that the church didn't approve of mixed couples going out together. The Reverend was my Sunday School teacher when I was a little kid and I was sure he wouldn't say anything bad about me. But I was wrong. It wasn't that he had anything against me personally. In fact, he told Mr. Baker what a fine young man I was and how I won the merit award in grade one at Bose Road Elementary, and what a fine future I had ahead of me. But going around with people of different colours was defying the word of God. The Reverend said that it was right in the Bible that people should stick to their own kind. He read some passages to Mary (from Deuteronomy, I think), and her father apparently seemed very pleased for Mary to get this little lecture.

After that we *really* had to sneak around. Sarah wasn't much help either. She'd see us down at Unwin Park and tell Mom. I was absolutely forbidden by my own mother to go out with my own girlfriend.

And Mr. Baker was going to come after me if he ever caught me out with her or heard that I'd been out with her.

Then I thought of a foolproof plan which I mentioned to Dickie while we were sitting in social studies. Mary and I would pretend that we had had a big fight and split up. She'd tell her dad that he was right about me.

She'd say that Dickie Williams (of whom her dad approved) liked her and he had asked her to skating and she had said that she would. When I asked Dickie if he would do it, he said, "You gotta be kidding. If I pick her up she's going out with me, that's for sure. I'm not lying to her old man just so you can sneak around with her. Why don't you pick her up yourself?"

"Very funny, Dickie. You know why. Her dad doesn't like me."

"Oh yeah. Why not?"

"He thinks I'm a bad influence on her, I guess."

"You—a bad influence. Yeah, right. I'm the one

who got pinched for stealing hubcaps and you're the bad influence."

"He doesn't like me because I'm coloured, and you know darn well. You just gotta go by and pick her up and I'll meet you down past Petersons. Then you can buzz off."

"Jiggers, here comes teach."

Mr. Higgins, our socials teacher, was coming down the aisle shaking his finger at me. "Why don't you just get out of my class if you want to talk, smart guy. We're supposed to be learning about your people today, not gossiping with Dickie Williams."

"My people, eh," I said, thinking: The closest I've ever been to Africa is Madrona Drive in Seattle.

So that's how it was with me and Dickie and Mary. He'd go by and call on her and if she was allowed out, I'd be waiting down Roebuck, just where the bushes are so thick that we'd be out of the view of anyone looking out the Bakers' windows. One night I waited out there for what must have been an hour, while Mrs. Baker served Dickie Kool-Aid and cookies. By the time they came out it was raining so hard that Mary had to run back to get her coat. But by then Dickie had gone home and Mr. Baker wanted to know why he didn't come back with her. He stuck his head out the door and called, "Dickie, Dickie Williams, come on in for a minute." But of course, no Dickie—which really must have pissed him off. So he decided he wouldn't let Mary go back out until Dickie came in. I was waiting around, even after it was dark. But Mary never did come out that night. What a hell of a way to have a girlfriend.

After that I started to spend less time with Mary and more time practising for the track team which I had joined because somebody figured I could turn out to be another Harry Jerome. I think it was Mr. Williams, the math teacher, who first got the bright idea.

Sarah and I went to see some real good movies, too. Mom wanted me to spend more time with Sarah because she didn't have many friends because as soon as somebody said something about her colour she might just punch them in the face.

Thinking about it now, I wish it hadn't happened, but I was even thinking about having a different girlfriend. I loved Mary, all right, and even though pulling all of those tricks on her parents might have been a bit of an adventure at first, after a while it wasn't really all that much fun, and even ruined a lot of the time we spent together.

I was a leader in Scouts two weeks after I joined up. Scoutmaster O'Reilly wanted to see me box because he had some idea that I'd be a natural. In fact, he promised me that I would get promoted just by going a round with Jamie Watson, who was not very tall but basically all muscles. Well, of course, Jamie punched me around pretty good, with me getting in exactly one good slug which wasn't as great an idea as a person might think, because it just made him want to do some real damage.

Mr. O'Reilly, even though extremely disappointed in me not turning out to be another Sugar Ray Robinson, kept his promise and promoted me to Scout leader. It turned out that there was a downside to that, too. Leaders get to do inspection line-ups which means inspecting if shoes are properly shined and neckties are properly tied and if fingernails are clean. That's how I came to be called a nigger for the first time. (I mean, by a white person.) Some coloured people, for some mysterious reason, think it's perfectly fine to call other coloured people "nigger" (for a joke, I guess), but if a white person does it they immediately want to see him dead and burning in hell as should happen to any scum of the earth.

Probably three years ago I was inspecting a line-up in Unwin Road hall, and I noticed that Jamie Watson, (the champ), hadn't polished his shoes properly.

"Get those shoes polished, Watson," I snarled as I went down the line-up, not really serious, just acting the drill sergeant role. Quiet enough that Scoutmaster O'Reilly couldn't hear, Jamie whispered, "I thought niggers were supposed to shine shoes. Wouldn't that be your job?"

I stood there staring at him, taken down off my high horse. Then another kid started chuckling as though Jamie had said something hilarious. That was my last day at Scouts. I remember taking off my green necktie and leaving it on the floor beside the side doors and getting out of there before Mr. O'Reilly could say anything.

After about three weeks without seeing Mary (except at school), I was walking by her place and she was sitting on her front porch again. Some people going by in a car had just yelled something at me so I wasn't in a great mood.

I stopped by the Baker's front gate for a minute and just stood there, not sure if Mr. Baker would be coming out and telling me not to hang around. Their car was gone so most likely he wasn't home.

Mary asked, "Did those guys in that car say something?"

"Yeah, something," I said, "but I don't know what it was. I think they said nigger. That makes about ten times now."

"Really?" she asked. "That many?"

"Like in Scouts. Remember I told you about that."

"Oh yeah, Jamie Watson, when you quit."

She came down from the front porch and we walked down to the back of the barn, then stood there leaning against the wall.

"Some people think it's funny yelling names out of cars," she said.

"I know."

"You still love me, though...right?" she asked, starting to smile.

"I don't know. Things aren't working out so great, are they."

"I know. But that's not our fault. People are just crazy."

"We should probably stop going out," I said, looking away.

Just then the Baker's car came down the road and went in the driveway so we walked down to the creek behind their place and sat on the planks that someone had put there for a bridge.

"So you want to break up, eh," she said, after a few minutes of just sitting there together, staring down into the water.

"I don't really want to, but what else are we going to do? Everybody's against it so much."

"Not everybody, just my dad."

"Not only him. The minister at Reidville Baptist even says it's not right—not to mention just about the whole United States of America."

"So?"

"That's a lot of people."

"What about getting married some day and everything?"

"Well, a lot of these people around here would sure have to change before that could ever happen."

"Jesus, Bill. So we're supposed to let other people run our lives, eh?"

"Well, if they weren't already we'd be sitting on your front porch instead of skulking around out here so nobody'll see us."

"Guess what, Bill?"

"What?"

"I missed my period."

"Huh?"

"Which means I could be pregnant."

I was shocked out of my skull. "You could be what? We only did it that one time. It takes a lot more than that."

"I don't think so. I thought you were smart in biology. Once is enough."

"That's really wonderful," I said. "I guess you know what your dad is going to think about that."

Goodbye, Billy Robinson! Holy Christ! What am I supposed to do now, shoot myself?

"He'll probably think it was Dickie if he finds out."

"*If*, eh. People tend to look different when they're pregnant, you know, so he'll probably get a rough idea sooner or later."

"Well...I'm only fourteen, so maybe he'll never know. There's doctors who can fix it, you know—if you can find one."

28

Then we heard her dad calling her from the back porch.

"I've got to get going, Bill. Do you still love me?"

"Of course I do, but I'm not sure that will help a lot."

Chapter 5

"You know, Billy, you're starting to get a complex about being a coloured boy."

"A what?" I said, sitting at the kitchen table, eating supper with Sarah.

Mom looked up from *Gone With The Wind*. "A complex," she repeated.

"Oh," I said. "What's that?"

"Don't you know what a complex is?" said Sarah. "I knew what that was when I was nine. Boy, are you ever dumb."

"I know what it is," I said.

"Eat your food, Sarah," interrupted Mom. "A complex is when you're always thinking about one thing. Can't you forget about your race for a while, Bill?"

"It's pretty hard, Mom. Every year since I started

31

school I've been the only coloured person except Sarah in the whole school."

"What about Xavier Wilty? He was in your class in grade four," said Sarah, looking at me as though I was lying.

"He's not coloured. He's Hawaiian or something," I said.

"You've got to stop thinking about it so much," said Mom.

"I don't think about it until somebody reminds me, like Jamie Watson telling me niggers should shine shoes. I bet you'd get a complex if somebody said that to you."

"You're going to have to learn not to let it bother you so much, son. You'll have to work it out. Sarah does."

"Yeah, but she works it out by smashing people in the face if they let anything slip about colour."

"I do not, Billy. You liar. How about you and Mary in the barn. I saw what you were doing."

Mom looked like she might faint at any second.

"Billy Robinson," she managed. "What were you and Mary doing?"

"Nothing, Mom. Sarah's just lying because I said she punches people."

Sarah didn't say anything after that, just stared at me, grinning. I got up and went outside before Mom could ask any more questions, then headed down to the creek feeling like the world was breathing down my back.

Probably Mom's favourite thing to do in the world was to get dressed up and take Sarah and I to church—before I quit going a couple of years ago. She had been raised in a community in a place called Wildwood, Alberta, which was full of people who figured the best way to get into heaven was to show up at church every Sunday dressed in their finest clothes. Judging from Mom, they weren't what you'd call "pious" but most of them would be quoting from the Bible a lot if any particular moral question should come up.

Grandpa, (Mom's dad) didn't quite believe the earth was round and I used to argue with him when he'd come over to bring us vegetables from his garden.

Of course grandpa never really listened to anything I had to say in the name of grade nine science, judging from the way he'd always cut me off in the middle of a sentence with his own version of everything.

"Sonny," he'd say, spitting into whatever it was we had fixed up for a spittoon, "those fancy flying machines ain't nothing but some riggin' they got in some

33

Hollywood studio and I'm a bit disappointed in you believing them Russians actually got dogs floating around up there in space."

Then we'd really argue until Mom got mad at me for being disrespectful—which usually came at the exact moment that I was winning the argument.

"There's enough disrespect in this world without you arguing with your grandfather, Bill. You're just being sassy."

That's when I decided to ask him about intermarriage—especially because our whole family was made up of a mixture of Seminole Indians, African slaves, Cree Indians and white people. So I was sure grandpa, whose first wife, Bessie, was the daughter of an African slave and a Seminole Indian, would have a pretty good opinion of it.

"Well, sonny, I'll tell ya. There's a scripture in the old testament that says that people should stick to their own kind." Which actually made me laugh as grandpa's parents certainly hadn't stuck to their own kind, considering the fact that he was probably the whitest black man alive anywhere. In fact, he didn't even look like a coloured man and people would have just thought he had a tan or was maybe Italian or Spanish.

"But aren't you a mixture, Grandpa? Wasn't grandmother Bessie part Seminole and part black?" I must have stumped him there for a minute because he didn't say a word, just shot another big gob of golden-brown chewing tobacco spit into the spittoon.

Finally he said, "Well, Billy. Have you ever noticed that black bulls don't go around white cows? You must have noticed *that.*"

Which was pretty well where I decided I couldn't compete very well with grandpa, especially with Mom accusing me of being disrespectful if it seemed that I was winning—or grandpa having a ready-made quote from the Bible that was guaranteed to win just about any argument we'd be having.

I love my grandfather, though. He's always watching out for us and bringing food down from his ranch at Lillooet, which is up in the Fraser Canyon. Like that time I wanted my own horse and he brought one down in the back of his truck. Unfortunately, the horse turned out to be "cut proud" which means that it wasn't really a gelding, as everyone thought, and was way too wild for anyone to handle, except real cowboys like grandpa. I eventually had to sell it at the auction in Cloverdale, which turned out to be the most humiliating thing in my life up to that point, as nobody wanted to buy the horse—only the fancy saddle that I had borrowed.

Chapter 6

A week or so after that last time in the hayloft, I was walking past Mary's house when Mr. Baker called me from the field where he was digging holes for fence posts.

"Hi, Mr. Baker," I yelled back, trying to be nonchalant.

"Billy Robinson, will you come here for a minute? I got something I want to talk to you about."

The sweat started dropping from my armpits.

"Uh...Mr. Baker...I uh...got to run an errand for my mother."

"This will only take a few minutes, Billy."

I imagined a quick death. Maybe a blow from his axe or a short wrestle with a police dog.

"Billy, c'mere, will you."

Mr. Baker was a great big man—at least six foot two. But I was sure he couldn't run as fast as I could. I walked down to the fence where he was working and stood a good fifteen feet away from him, leaning on a fence post.

"Billy, are you afraid of me?" said the giant man whose only daughter I had knocked up.

"Whadya want, Mr. Baker? I got to go to the store for my mom."

"Bill, you like Mary quite a bit, don't you?"

"Yessir, she's a pretty nice girl."

"I guess you think you might marry her when you're older, eh?"

"Oh no, sir. We never talked about anything like *that*."

"Well, Bill, I thought I'd tell you before you get any such ideas. We don't believe in it in our family."

"My grandpa says it's one of the worst things you can do," I said.

"Well, he's right, you know, Bill. It's a pretty terrible thing. The children suffer. Half black and half white. People hating them everywhere they turn."

"I guess so, Mr. Baker."

"I don't want you to think I got anything against you people. I think your mother's a very fine woman. And your sister's the best babysitter we ever had. But it's you and Mary I'm thinking about. I don't want you making plans for something that can never happen. I was young once myself, so I know how it can be."

38

"Well, thanks, sir, I..."

"I just thought you should know how it is. That way we won't have any misunderstandings."

"Well, thanks again. I guess I should get up to the store now."

"How old are you now, Bill?"

"Fifteen."

"I guess you get kind of, uh...horny sometimes, eh, son?"

"Mr. Baker?" I figured this was it. He dropped his tools and looked straight at me.

"I think you know what I mean. You'd like to sleep with Mary, wouldn't you?"

"Mr. Baker, I..."

"No use hidin' it, son. Mary's an awful pretty girl. But let me tell you one thing, Bill. Don't you ever do it, 'cause if I ever find out you and Mary have been foolin' around I'll come after you. You hear me?"

"Yessir. I got to go now." I turned and started walking away.

"You remember that, Billy," he called after me.

I didn't get to see Mary for a week or so after that little talk with her dad. She was off picking beans down in Ladner and I was helping Sarah cut Cascara bark in the woods. (They make medicine out of it). That was

39

a pretty good way to make a few extra dollars. We stripped the bark from Cascara trees and sold it to the Co-op in potato sacks for about sixteen cents a pound, which was fairly decent money.

So there we were stripping bark and something's coming through the bush making a hell of a racket.

"It could be a bear, Billy. Let's get going. I'm scared."

"Naw, Sarah, there's no bears around here. It's just a big dog."

Then our neighbour, Mr. Hoffman, came trudging through the bush.

"Hey, you pickaninnies, what are you doing stripping bark from my trees? Stay on your own property. What's the matter? Strip all your own trees, already?" He was carrying his old Cooey shotgun.

"We're only trying to make a few bucks for school's all," I yelled. "We only did a couple of trees."

My voice was unsteady as I eyed the gun. But I was sure tired of being pushed around by white men. I threw my bag of bark at him, grabbed Sarah's hand, and took off running back down the trail towards the house.

In those days it seemed like I was always running for something or from somebody. I guess that's how I got to be such a good runner. If I wasn't running from somebody making me feel bad about my colour, I was running to win races at school. It wasn't that I particularly liked running or anything, but it sure was a good way to solve problems. But getting Mary pregnant! Wow! There was no place to run from that. If her dad didn't get me the Mounties would. But honestly, I really didn't know what to do about it. I couldn't tell anybody. I mean, there wasn't anybody I could tell that I'd knocked up a fourteen-year-old girl. And a white girl, too—which was twice as bad. Normally I would have gone to talk to the minister about it like I did a couple times with other things. Like the time Dickie and I were caught smashing up a bunch of Mr. Hoffman's pumpkins, or when me and my cousin Eddie stole those cherries. But this was something *big* and the Reverend wasn't on my side anyway. Then I got the dumb idea to see if Dickie would take the rap for me.

"Look Billy, everybody's gonna find out sooner or later anyway. You might as well fess up now. If her old man ever finds out she's pregnant, he's going to go after somebody. It might as well be you. I'm too young."

"Listen, Dickie, you gotta do this for me. You don't have to say you knocked her up. I just want you *not* to say you didn't so Mr. Baker'll think maybe you did."

"He won't be able to come after me 'cause he won't have any way of knowing if I did it for sure. Or else poof! Goodbye Billy Robinson."

"Kee-riste, Bill, I seen this movie where some guy got a girl in trouble and he just got a bunch of his friends to say that they *all* made out with her. Nobody could do nothing about it 'cause they couldn't figure out who the real father was."

"You trying to make a slut outta Mary, Dickie? She loves me, you know. She's not like that."

"What makes you so sure? She went out with me a few times, you know."

"How would you like a good smack in the mouth, Dickie?"

"Aw, don't go and get sore. I'm only kidding."

I stopped pedalling and got off my bike and leaned against it, gazing down the road at Mary's bedroom window.

"You know, Dickie, there's just no way I can get out of it."

"Why not, Bill?"

"'Cause I'm coloured."

"Aw, come on. You just think everybody's picking on you. You ain't the first guy who ever got a girl pregnant, you know."

"I'm not saying *that*. I mean…it's not fair. If I was white, I'd just say it wasn't me and nobody would ever know, but I'm the only coloured guy in this part of Canada. Talk about discrimination!"

Mary seemed to love me, all right. At least I didn't have to worry about that. She even said we could run away and elope, or something, if her dad threatened me. But at least I wasn't *that* dumb. They'd find us in a few hours, anyway. Where's a fifteen-year-old coloured boy and a fourteen-year-old white girl going to hide? I mean...we'd be recognized right away and turned in.

Mom and Sarah couldn't help either. In fact, I was afraid to tell them because if they knew they'd want to go and sit down with the Bakers and talk the whole thing out. But you couldn't talk to Mr. Baker democratically. As soon as he got mad, he'd want to do something violent.

Chapter 7

A couple of weeks before school started Dickie and I took Marabelle and Mary hiking up in Garibaldi Park. Dickie picked up Mary, of course, while I waited down behind the barn. Everything was going fine, walking down the trail away from the barn with Dickie and Mary. It was a great day. The whole world was kind of opening up like spring. Only it wasn't spring. I wish I knew how to describe nature better 'cause for a while that morning with Dickie and Mary I felt that maybe everything would pass; that I'd be able to really enjoy the weather and things like that again. Mary looked so pretty. She had on this pretty yellow dress with some kind of sash tied around her waist. I think it's called Bavarian or something, where her parents are from in Germany. I picked a flower for her hair and she wore it all day.

We went up Roebuck towards Marabelle's place and met her standing up the road about two blocks from her driveway.

"I didn't want my dad to see you, Billy. He's kind of prejudiced," said Marabelle sweetly, almost ruining the whole trip before it got started. Even worse, when we got on the bus, Mr. Hoffman was sitting right there in the front seat, talking to the bus driver.

"Hi there, Billy boy. Now don't forget to go right to the back of the bus." Then he laughed like it was real funny.

Was I ever embarrassed for Mary to hear people saying things like that to me. I felt like running and hiding down by the creek.

That could have been a really great day. Dickie and Marabelle sat in the second seat from the front and Mary and I sat right behind them. Every once in a while she'd turn to me and kiss me and say she loved me or something like that. But I was mostly just trying to think of something to do about her being pregnant, and staring at Mr. Hoffman, wishing I had the nerve to walk up the aisle and punch him right in the mouth and call him a dirty prejudiced son of a bitch.

It was really pretty up at Whonnock Lake. The water was so blue. Dickie rented a rowboat and the four of us went swimming off the boat and horsing around, having a very good time. For a while I forgot

46

about everything. Mary and I swam over to a little island with about ten trees on it and a tiny lawn of bright green grass and watched Dickie and Marabelle diving from the boat.

"The sky's so blue, Bill." She was lying down looking up at me. "Maybe the baby will have blue eyes like that."

"I don't think so. My grandpa says brown is dominant."

"Dominant? What's *that*?" she asked, seeming disappointed.

"It means that when brown people and white people make a baby together, the baby will look like a mixture—half and half—but eye colour comes from the darker person—in this case, me."

Mary looked away. "You mean it's going to be a Negro baby."

"I don't know. Everybody'll probably call it a coloured baby."

"Why should they? It'll be just as much white as black."

"What's the difference, Mary? Do you really care that much?"

"Oh, Bill, don't be so sensitive. I don't care what colour it is as long as everybody doesn't hate it."

I guess Mary had been listening to her dad talking a bunch of crap about being half white and half black.

"Aw, Mary, don't believe your dad's bullshit. He's just prejudiced."

"He doesn't know I'm going to have a baby."

"I know that, but don't believe what he says about people of mixed races being hated by everybody."

"He says they'll be hated by white people and coloured people because they don't belong to either side. He knew a half-white girl back on the prairies and she didn't have any friends. In fact, her own parents kicked her out of the house just because she was part coloured."

"And you believe that crap?" I said, getting pissed off. "He's just making stuff up because he wants you to believe a bunch of lies."

"He says that they're a lot dumber than all white or all coloured, too, and that a lot of them are deformed."

"You know, Mary, your dad's a fucking idiot."

I was sitting up staring at the water. Then that same old feeling of not wanting her to see how bad I felt about all of this came back.

Every time we talked about race there was this really strong feeling to run and hide somewhere. Sitting there with my back to her was kind of like hiding, and when she reached up to pull me down on the grass I pushed her away gently, which must have hurt her feelings because she just got up and ran into the lake saying she'd race me over to the boat. Dickie

48

and Marabelle were having such a great time fooling around in the water and diving from the boat. They hardly even noticed that Mary and I weren't so happy.

In the afternoon we bought some fries and pop and hiked up the hill through the woods away from the lake to look for a secluded place to have a picnic. Marabelle was really playing up to Dickie and he was enjoying it. She'd let her bathing suit top slide down her shoulder and get him to fix it for her. Up the hill we found a small grassy clearing where they took off laughing, chasing a brown rabbit that popped out from the bush. They disappeared into a little thicket and soon all the laughing and giggling stopped. "I wonder what they're doing," said Mary, kind of slyly, stretching out under a maple tree. "Dickie's sure making a hit with her, eh."

"Seems that way." I lay down beside her and picked a bluebell for her.

"Mary, you're going to love our baby, aren't you?" I asked, which was weird because I didn't mean to be so serious.

She sat up, taking my hands in hers. "Why would you ever have to wonder about that?"

"Because in this lousy world people make me wonder about things like that all the time. They don't let you ever forget. Like Mr. Hoffman, telling me to go right to the back of the bus. Very funny! He's just like your old man..."

49

She got up and walked a few feet down the path and I followed her, not wanting her to be mad at me because things *could* have been great. She was so pretty.

"Can we not talk about it today, Billy? Marabelle and Dickie don't sit around arguing all day. They're having so much fun...and look at us, just moping around, thinking about what my dad's going to do when he finds out."

I put my arms around her waist and we just stood like that for a minute until the rabbit that Dickie and Marabelle had been chasing ran out from the bush and sat staring at us. He was chewing with that funny mouth movement that rabbits have. When we knelt down he hopped away, but he didn't go far. I wanted to see how close I could get to him so I followed, crawling towards him. He'd retreat a few feet and I'd stop, motionless, hoping he wouldn't disappear into the bush. But for some strange reason he preferred the lawn and he didn't really hide at all. He was eating flowers while keeping an eye on me to see how close I was. Mary went back to lie under the trees while I crawled around trying to sneak up on the rabbit. Finally it took off, hopping towards the trees, and I gave up. When I stood up, I spotted Dickie and Marabelle lying just off the trail—probably as close together as two people could ever get.

Chapter 8

The next Monday was Labour Day and school would start up again Tuesday. Sarah and I had almost fifty dollars saved up from stripping Cascara bark and picking beans. Mom was sending us to Seattle to go shopping with Aunt Elsie because almost everything is way cheaper down there. I didn't really want to go because I'd have to leave Mary and I wanted to see her Monday night so we could talk about school. But Mom wouldn't let me stay home so Sarah and I got on the Great Northern train at White Rock. I don't remember too much about that train ride because I was mostly staring out the window and thinking about Mary, and besides, I'd been on trains before. Our dad's a sleeping car porter on the CPR and once before he took us to work with him all the way to Winnipeg. But I *do* remember watching the porters and thinking about what my dad looked like when he was working. Man, I sure didn't figure him for one of these guys... bowing and scraping, saying yessir and no sir. The porter even called me sir. I don't know what I thought my dad did on the train but I hadn't thought of him saying yessir to little kids. And then there was that one guy who called the porter (who must have been fifty years old) "boy." The porter just smiled and said: "I's a comin', boss" as a joke—which didn't seem very funny to me.

Seattle wasn't any better. Sarah didn't notice as much as I did, probably because she'd lived in Minneapolis for one summer, but all the black people in Seattle seem to live in one part of town and hardly ever speak to white people unless they absolutely have to. It's hard to explain, but white people look at a person different down there, too—as though they think you're not quite human or something. Most of the time they don't even seem to notice you. Aunt Elsie met us at the train station in her '56 Crown Victoria, which is a Ford. She's a big fat lady, about two-hundred-and-fifty pounds, I bet. Sarah really thought that was great—driving around town with Aunt Elsie who was talking as though she had just found her two lost babies. "William," she said, "when are you going to do something about that hair? I told your mom about that. The young men down here are using permastraight, now. They look so fine. You're a regular little fuzzball."

"Whadya mean?" I asked, totally bewildered. I didn't know there was something wrong with my hair.

"Soon's we're done shopping I'm going to take you over to see Sammy so he can show you how to take care of your hair."

Sarah got a lot of dresses and shoes for school and I got track and soccer shoes, jeans, a ton of underwear and a jacket at the Bon Marché which we got at a discount as Aunt Elsie works there washing floors. Then we went over to see Sammy, the barber, who pissed me off by insisting that my hair just *had* to be straightened if I was going to look like a proper young man. Sometimes I don't know what's wrong with people. It seems like the coloured people in Seattle are doing everything they can so no one will notice that they're not white.

Aunt Elsie said that down in Mississippi, where she'd lived before her husband died, they've got signs in front of all the stores and restaurants saying whether they're for black people or white people. And the police enforce it too! That was the part that really pissed me off. What are police for if not to stop crimes like that? The United States is totally insane, but they don't seem to notice it. I tried to imagine what it would feel like being kept out of places because you're the wrong colour, but I couldn't. In the park across the street from Aunt Elsie's house there was a baseball game going on and not one single guy was white. Everybody was having a great time, all right, but it seemed so weird that only coloured kids played there—like they were animals, or something, separated off from the rest of the human race. Maybe Mom was right. Maybe I *was* getting a complex about being coloured. That night Aunt Elsie made us stuff called chit'lins with cornbread and spare ribs and we had it on the front veranda and watched everything that was going on over in the park. To me, it was like some new kind of world. Coloured people everywhere! I had never seen so many coloured people all in the same place, except in *National Geographic* magazine and shows where white people go on safaris.

After dinner, Sarah and I walked down to a little café called Rosie's to get milkshakes. It was the kind of place they'd call a "greasy spoon" back home. There were so many people in there that you could hardly move. And they were all coloured people, too. Sarah sat down in a booth while I ordered at the counter. Everybody was really friendly, but boy, were they ever different! The jukebox was turned way up high and two couples were dancing, doing a dance called the "dirty boogie." A bunch of guys were crowded around a pinball machine and whooping every time something happened on the machine. When our shakes were ready, we left in a hurry, glad to get away from there.

On the way back to Aunt Elsie's I was thinking that it sure was a different kind of experience being in Seattle. I mentioned that to Sarah and she agreed, but I think she was kind of shocked by the whole thing and didn't have the words to express how she felt.

We caught the train for Newton the next morning and Sarah let me sit beside the window all the way home. I guess she was trying to be nice because she could see that I wasn't very happy. That's one good thing that came out of the trip to Seattle. I found out that Sarah could be a pretty nice sister. We even talked about Mary. She said that from now on she wouldn't be babysitting for Mary's little brother because Mr. Baker was so prejudiced against me. Of course I didn't mention anything to her about Mary being pregnant because even though she seemed to have turned over a new leaf in Seattle, I was sure she'd go blab everything to Mom as soon as she got mad at me for something—which was sure to happen sooner or later.

The ride home was very quiet. I looked out the window most of the time and thought about how pretty Mary could look—especially in that yellow dress with the Bavarian sash around her waist. I even mailed her a postcard telling her about the track shoes and riding in Aunt Elsie's Ford. I really wanted to tell her how much I missed her but probably her dad would get the mail and read it, so I didn't mention it.

Chapter 9

"Promise you'll never leave me again, forever and ever."

That was almost the first thing Mary said to me when I met her down by the creek. I promised all right, but I sure never knew how I was going to keep my promise with things going so rotten. I might have to go away and live with my relatives in St. Paul. But I didn't say anything to her about that. We sat down on a log and and I tossed rocks into the water. I didn't feel like kissing or anything, though. And neither did she.

"Bill," she said, chucking a couple of rocks, "do you think we'd ever be able to get married? Maybe we could put the baby in a home until we're old enough. Then we could have him ourselves."

Wow! That was just too much for me to think about all at once.

"Your dad says they don't believe in it in his family."

"Believe in what—adoption?"

"No, intermarriage."

She just sat there for a minute without saying anything. Then she said, "You know, Billy Robinson, sometimes you act just like a baby yourself. Can't you stop worrying about my dad and start thinking about me and the baby? He's not going to be running my life forever, you know."

She was right, of course. I *was* immature and probably not even acting my age. I'd been so afraid of what everyone was going to say that I had hardly given a single thought to what she was going through.

"We've got to make some kind of plans, you know," she said. "We can't just sit around and wait for things to happen without saying anything to anybody." She was getting pretty upset so I put my arms around her. Did I ever feel at a loss, though. I had forgotten that we had to do something about it.

"I don't know what we're going to do about it," I said. "But we've got to think of something. Maybe I'll tell a teacher and see what he thinks. That's the only thing I can think of."

"Yeah," she said. "The students' counsellor should know what to do—Miss Abercrombie. They've got homes for unwed mothers where you can go and live until you have the baby. Then they'll find a good home for it. You can just tell everybody that you went to live with relatives so nobody will ever know."

"Could you ever do that?" I asked, surprised.

"I might have to. You could come visit on the weekends."

"Think so? Would that be allowed?"

"I can't see why not. I bet it would."

Imagine! Mary was younger than me and she was trying to give *me* confidence—instead of the other way around. She seemed to be growing up fast all of a sudden. I've heard it said that girls mature faster than boys and judging by her new attitude there must be something to it. For a few days after that I was feeling a bit better about things. At least we were trying to figure something out.

Chapter 10

Princess Margaret is one of the smallest high schools around. It had never had any great athletes to speak of and had never even gotten into the BC championships until two years ago when a couple of the guys made a very good showing in several events. "Another Harry Jerome," Mr. Willard said about me, when he introduced his new "track stars" to the assembly. Even though I hadn't come in first in any of the events, he was counting on me to get at least one gold ribbon at the next track meet. We had a few preliminary races soon after the first day of school but for some strange reason the best I could do was fourth in the hundred yards and third in broad jump. Nobody was even close to this new kid, Barry Wakefield, and Mr. Willard didn't try very hard to hide how disappointed he was in me. Being compared to Harry Jerome was one of the high points of my life up to that time, but nobody ever mentioned it again.

To keep up my side of the bargain I had with Mary, I decided to talk to a teacher about our problem. The same day that I'd lost my title as a school track star, I went up to see Mr. Higgins, our social studies teacher. When I peeked through the open door I could see him standing on a chair, putting up posters.

"Hi, Bill," he said, pushing thumb tacks into the wall.

"Can I see you for a minute, sir?" I asked, trying to figure out what the posters were all about.

"Sure, Bill, how's it going? Funny you should come along just now. I was just thinking about you."

"You were?" I asked, astonished.

"I'm starting a new study program this year and I'm hoping you'd like to be involved."

"I've always like social studies, sir."

"Well, I'm thinking it might be a good idea to have a few students do a report on their background and present it to the class.What's *your* family's background, Bill? Where are your people from?"

"Mostly Florida and Oklahoma, but my mother was born in Edmonton."

"Not your relatives, Bill. I mean your ancestors. Do you know?"

"Well, I guess a lot of them were slaves from Africa," I said, starting to feel embarrassed.

"Do you know what part of Africa?"

"Not really. People didn't keep very good records in those days. All's I know is a lot of them lived with Seminole Indians when they escaped from plantations. My grandfather married a Seminole girl—stole her in the middle of the night."

"Really, Bill, that's quite a story."

"There were thousands of runaway slaves in Florida, sir. They had their own town and everything. They even had a war with the American army."

"They did? I never heard about that, Bill."

"Well, it's not commonly known. My grandpa says they keep it out of textbooks on purpose."

"On purpose? Why would they do that?"

"My grandpa says to make coloured people look like they were too afraid to fight for their own freedom like everybody else had to. Like in all the Hollywood movies they make all the coloured people look like they're really dumb—like fools or clowns, like Stepin Fetchit and Amos and Andy."

Mr. Higgins looked out the window for a minute. Then he said, "That's very interesting, Bill. I'm going to have to look that up. Their own town, eh. Really?"

"That's what my grandfather says. His dad lived in the town. It was in Florida—in the swamplands. After the war with the American army they ended up in Oklahoma in the Indian Territories."

"You know, Bill. I've never heard about slaves having towns or fighting a war with the American army in Florida. Where'd you learn all of this stuff?"

"My grandfather. He talks about it a lot."

"Well, if it's all true it has to be in the library. I'll look it up."

"It's not in books, sir."

"Uh...well, do you think you'd like to do a report on it for the class? It's very interesting. I thought you and Jimmy Takahashi could work together. He's doing one on Japan. Maybe bring in pictures and talk about the history."

Mr. Higgins was looking really enthusiastic about this. I guess I was frowning or something because he suddenly said that it wouldn't be that hard and that he'd help me write it if I wanted him to and that if it was really good I could give it in front of the whole school at assembly.

"Mr. Higgins, I..."

"Well, just let me know, Bill. There's no hurry. Ask your folks. Looks like your grandfather would have a lot of background stuff—*and* a lot of fascinating stories you could use."

I don't know what made me say it—like I had another person inside of me—but Mr. Higgins was smiling at me and I guess that struck a nerve or something. I blurted out, "Mr. Higgins, I don't want to be useful to the class. I came in here to talk to you about something and you just want to use me for a teaching aid."

"Billy?" he said, probably as shocked as I was by the way it came out.

"And I'm not taking geography this year, either."

Then I was running again, across the schoolyard and down Roebuck, towards home. It was really weird how all of that stuff came out. Especially me telling Mr. Higgins all about slavery because anytime I think about it it just makes me mad. Even the word pisses me off—whoever's saying it.

Chapter 11

"If this was the South, Bill, things would be a lot different. But Canadians are better than *that*. And you're only fifteen so you're too young to be prosecuted for it."

Mr. Willard was talking like he knew exactly what he was talking about.

"You know, Billy, there's almost no prejudice against you people in Canada. But a lot of people—and I guess I go along with them—don't believe in mixing the races."

"I know," I said.

Mr. Willard put his papers down and walked around to the side of his desk.

"You know, Billy," he said, "I'm glad you came to me with this problem because I really think a lot of people would advise you wrongly. But I'm used to this kind of thing. Well, not exactly, *this* kind of thing, but being a counsellor, quite a few guys have come to tell me that they've gotten girls in trouble over the years."

Which made me feel, for a minute, that I had done the right thing in coming to Mr. Willard.

"Billy, what I have always told them is to get together with everybody concerned—the girl, her parents, and your parents, and try to work out the best thing for everybody, including the baby."

"It's not that easy, sir."

"I know that, Bill. Your case is a bit different."

At least Mr. Willard understood *that.*

"That's one thing I learned a long time ago, counselling athletes," he said. "You can't have one pat answer for everybody."

"That's for sure, sir."

"Being a person of mixed race is one of the most difficult problems a person can have, Bill. On the one hand it's more likely that a mixed person will have brain damage or be feeble-minded or physically deformed. On the other hand, if the child does manage to be normal physically and mentally, there's the full gamut of hatred and disapproval to run. It's like belonging to two worlds, but being accepted by neither."

"Oh," I said. I wanted to say that I'd heard it all before, but Mr. Willard would have been insulted. He sounded like he was at last making the speech that he'd saved up for a long time.

"Billy, I think the best thing for you to do is see if you can find a doctor who will perform an abortion."

I was so shocked by what he said that I could hardly believe my ears.

"An abortion, sir?" I hardly knew what that was.

"Yes, Billy, I think it's the best thing all around."

"Yeah, but aren't they against the law?" I said, trying out what little knowledge I had on the subject.

"Bill, during the Hitler years in Germany, it was against the law for Jews to even be alive. Some laws just aren't fair."

I thought of those signs in Mississippi which said: FOR WHITES ONLY. Neither of us said a word for a few seconds.

"I think I'll go now, sir." I turned to leave and he called me back.

"Bill, I'd appreciate it if you don't tell anybody about this. There are a lot of prejudiced people around here."

"No, sir. I won't."

"Tell me what you decide to do, son."

"Okay, Mr. Willard. Thanks a lot."

Wow! I sure didn't know what to think after Mr. Willard said *that*. I could kind of see what he meant about some laws not being fair and everything. But I didn't know enough about abortion to decide if it should be illegal or not. I tried thinking about it but I

69

just got all boggled up. And even if it was a good idea, how was I ever going to find a doctor to do it? Mr. Willard sure liked to hear himself talk, but when it came down to actually helping somebody with something, he was a total blank.

Mr. Baker wouldn't let Mary even walk to school with me. She said he asked her. "What will the neighbours think, seeing you walking with that little nigger every day?" So I had to wait until noon to see her. I never did tell her what Mr. Willard had said about her having an abortion. Maybe it was because I was afraid she'd think it was a good idea and try to get me to help her find a doctor who'd do it. And I knew that was absolutely impossible.

Neither of us was doing very well in school. Mr. Gibbons gave us a test on set theory, which is the new math, and I didn't get one single question right. That new math is sure hard if you don't listen to what's going on. And Mary didn't do much better on her first test. She said she was six weeks pregnant. We had to do something pretty soon. To see if I could figure something out I took the bus to New Westminster to find something on abortion in the big library. Sarah wanted to come with me but I told her I was going to the YMCA and she wouldn't be allowed to come inside. It was kind of funny to find out that it is actually legal to have an abortion in some countries, but not in

Canada. I never could figure out how each country could have its own set of laws and expect everybody to think that they were the best. I mean, somebody must be wrong! In Japan, lots of girls have abortions. All they have to do is go to a doctor and say: Can I please have an abortion? And the doctor will do it. Simple as that. But in Canada a doctor can go to jail for doing the same thing. So I came home from the library feeling more confused about abortions than ever.When I got home I waited for dark, then went over to the Bakers' barn where me and Mary had plans to meet at nine o'clock. As luck would have it, I happened to glance through the window when I went past the house and I could see Mr. Baker spanking Jimmy on the behind.

Jimmy was crying as though he was really getting hurt. Then I heard Mary call my name from a little clump of trees behind the barn.

"Over here," she called. I couldn't see her at first but then she moved and I caught sight of her. When I got over to her she took my hand and we ran down the trail away from the barnyard. "The trees smell so nice," she said when we stopped running. Then she let go of my hand and went over and grabbed a maple branch that was hanging down low. Still hanging on, she twirled around it a couple of times and ended up looking up at the moon. She sure was pretty! I didn't ask why Jimmy was in trouble right away, as it would have stopped her fooling around like that. She'd never played around like that before in the woods. The moon was extra bright, too.

"How come Jimmy's in trouble?" I finally asked. She didn't answer so I didn't ask her again right then.

"You know, Bill, this is probably the most beautiful place in the world, I bet. Look at the moon. It's *so* bright."

"Yeah, I know," I said.

"Slowly, silently, now the moon walks the night in its silver shoon," she said.

Which I recognized from Walter de la Mare's poem, "Silver."

"Keep going," I said.

She let go of the branch and just stood there. I remember that whole scene just like it was yesterday.

When she finally came over to where I was lying on the moss she had tears on her face.

"Billy, sometimes I wish you weren't a Negro," she said. That was sure a funny thing to say. I guess it made me kind of mad, so I didn't say anything, only looked at her like she had hurt my feelings (which she had).

"Marabelle and Dickie don't have to worry about her dad hating him on account of his colour."

"Of course not. He's the right colour." Which was supposed to be funny, but Mary didn't laugh. I wanted to love her *so* much, but when I thought about what she had said for a second it bothered me even more. I couldn't help what colour I was.

"For Christ's sake, Mary. I can't help it what colour I am, you know. What am I supposed to do? Paint my-self white?" I stood up and took a couple of steps away from her. Then I felt like running.

"Sorry, Bill," she said. "I didn't mean to hurt your feelings. I just wish everybody didn't hate you so much, that's all."

"Everybody doesn't hate me. I've got *lots* of friends." Saying this almost made me cry, and for a second I thought I would, so I got up and walked away, just in case. I was standing in the dark, behind a cedar, out of the light from the moon. Mary sat there, squinting into the darkness.

"I can't see you. Are you hiding on me, now?" she asked.

"I guess I'm just too dark for you to see," I said, suddenly thinking it was funny. That really made her laugh and she came over and leaned against the tree with me. We stood there hugging for quite a while until I thought about Jimmy getting a spanking.

"How come Jimmy's getting a spanking?" I asked. "Your dad looked *really* mad."

"How did you find out about that?"

"When I went by the side of the house I happened to look in the window."

73

She looked away for a few seconds then she said, "Because he said he saw us making out up in the loft."

"What? Are you kidding? That's not very funny, you know. You mean that *one* night? How would he see us? Oh great!"

"He said he climbed up the ladder."

"He got a spanking for *that*?"

"I said he was lying and they believed me. At least my dad did."

"Jesus Christ! As if we don't have enough to worry about." I sat down on a log and started fooling with a stick, stabbing it into the ground. Mary came and sat beside me.

"I wish I hadn't lied," she said.

"Yeah, well every time we see each other we have to lie about it, or your dad will go nuts."

"I know." Then she stood up and walked a few steps away. "Billy," she said. "I don't want to sneak around any more. And I'm getting tired of lying all the time." She was standing with her back to me. I remember thinking this was just like *Romeo and Juliet* or something. When she turned around there were tears on her face. "Do you know what he said? He said if I was making love to you it would be just like fucking an animal."

Chapter 12

I didn't tell anybody what Mr. Baker had said because actually I was too embarrassed. I didn't even tell Dickie. But it was sure an awful thing to say to a fourteen-year-old girl. When Mary told her mother what he had said her mother got choked too, and she really told him off, which I was glad to know. There were a lot of funny feelings running through my mind. After I left Mary that night I had this plan run through my brain where I would shoot Mr. Baker through the window. That was just a stupid fantasy, of course. I didn't know how to shoot a gun, let alone Mr. Baker. Then I got the idea to just march right up their front steps and knock on the door and tell Mr. Baker that I had come to call on his daughter to take her out skating or something. And I might even say that she was pregnant, too, and that what Jimmy said was true, and that I was proud of it. That would sure fix him!

Mary's mother didn't seem to hate me as much as her dad. At least she never called me names or told Mary lies about coloured people. She just said that Mr. Baker was the head of the household and as long as Mary lived under his roof she would have to abide by his rules. It was really hard to figure out if Mary's mother was a bit prejudiced or not, but that night I got to thinking that maybe she would be the best one to know that Mary was pregnant. Anyway, Mary was more than six weeks gone by then and somebody had to know. Somebody had to help her take care of herself so she wouldn't get sick or let the baby get sick even before it was born.

Sunday morning I was up early walking in the pasture full of those yellow flowers that people hold under your chin and ask if you like butter or not... buttercups. The sun was already hot and I kicked up the dust as I stepped along, thinking how beautiful and good my life could have been if people weren't so full of hatred. I didn't know exactly what I was going to do that morning, but I was kind of watching the Baker farm down the road. They'd be going to church pretty soon and I guess I just wanted to see them so I could maybe get some idea what to do. I couldn't help thinking what a hypocrite Mr. Baker was—taking his family to church to worship the same god that I used to believe in. I told Mom about that and she said that that was nothing—

that down South the white preachers preach the brotherhood of man to all-white congregations. Mary was leaning out of her window at the top of the house. As soon as she saw me in the field she started waving and I waved back but just then Mr. Baker came out onto the front porch, and for some strange reason looked right at me leaning against a fence post. That really made me mad. I couldn't even wave to my own girlfriend without getting in trouble. Suddenly I started waving real hard at Mary. I don't know what made me do it, but I just wanted Mr. Baker to see that I wasn't afraid of him (which I was). It was a very strange thing; Mary could see me but she couldn't see her dad, and he could see me, but he couldn't see Mary. I could see both of them. Pretty soon Mr. Baker came down from the porch, walked around to the side of the house and looked up at Mary who was throwing me kisses from her bedroom window.

I heard him say, "Mary, what do you think you're doing, flirting with that nigger?" Then he stomped back around the front again and met Mrs. Baker and Jimmy. They all climbed into the car and took off up the street on the way to church. As soon as the car turned the corner I started to run towards Mary's house, but then I just stopped running and stood there watching her wave to me. Then I got a bit dizzy—probably from all the excitement of standing up to Mr. Baker, and the sun beating down on me like that. I didn't feel too good at all. I sat down against a post and looked up at Mary's window. She was gone. Some ants were climbing up my pants. They sure weren't afraid of anything. Mary was running towards me, kicking up the dust as she came.

"Hi, Bill," she said, walking up to where I was sitting against the post.

"How come you didn't go to church?" I asked, looking up at her. She was standing between the sun and me so I couldn't see her face very well.

"Because I don't believe in it anymore, that's why."

"Yeah, me neither—'specially with the kind of people they let in there."

She didn't say anything for a while, just stood there with a strange look on her face, which made me think I might have hurt her feelings. Finally she blurted out, "My dad's not the worst person in the world, you know. In some places you could get lynched for just whistling at a white girl, let alone what we did."

That was sure a surprise for her to be saying this, as if she was trying to make excuses for her dad or something. "Is that right?" I said. "How do *you* know?"

She came and sat down with me on the ground. "My mom told me about Emmett Till last night," she said, sounding really sad.

"Who?"

"Emmett Till."

"Who's he?"

"He was a coloured boy from Chicago. He went down South to spend the summer with his cousins and some men killed him for whistling at a white girl in a grocery store."

"Really?" I asked. "I don't believe it. They're just making up stuff to scare you. I don't believe it. I woulda heard about *that*. When did *that* happen?"

"Four or five years ago. They tortured him, then they shot him and threw him in the river."

"I still don't believe it," I said, getting pretty upset.

"Well, it's true."

"How do you know?"

"Because my mom's got it in a magazine. She showed me."

"How old was he?"

"Fourteen."

"Fucking bastards. Did they catch the guys that did it?"

"Yeah, they caught them, but nothing happened to them."

"How could nothing happen to them if they caught them?"

"There was a trial and everything, but they got off. The jury wouldn't convict them."

"Wouldn't convict them? How come?"

"They do it all the time down there."

"Do what?"

"Kill coloured guys for flirting with white women. My mom's got pictures of a lynching. Even the little kids are laughing at the coloured man who's hanging from a tree—like it's all a big joke."

"Are you sure? The *kids* are laughing?"

"Yup. Like they're having a big picnic."

"Where'd you see *that*?"

"*Look* magazine. My mom saved it. I can show you."

"No thanks," I said. "So now you think your dad's not so bad, eh."

"I dunno."

"If he was down there he'd probably be joining right in."

I could tell that Mary didn't like me saying this. She stood up and walked over to another post. "No he wouldn't," she said. "He wouldn't do *that*."

"I dunno. He sure hates my guts, that's for sure."

"Hey, Bill, we should go down to the creek. Everybody can see us here."

"So what? They won't be back 'til at least noon. Besides, I'm not running and hiding anymore."

I guess I sounded a bit pissed off when I said that and she started walking away.

"I'm sorry, Mary," I called after her. "I'll go down to the creek if you want."

"Never mind, Bill. I'm not supposed to be with

80

TRUMAN GREEN

you and you're not running and hiding anymore—re-member?"

I really wanted to catch up with her and hug her but I couldn't do it. I just sat there in the field tossing little rocks at the flowers. Then I got up and *walked* down to the creek by myself.

I guess I should have talked to my mother or at least Sarah about Mary being pregnant, but I could just imagine how they'd take it—especially my mother. It was more than just being afraid of what would happen to me if Mr. Baker found out. I started to think I had to stop running away from everything. That thing with Emmett Till really bugged me, too. How could they kill a kid for whistling at somebody? Even if the bastards were prejudiced they didn't have to kill him.

The next time I saw Mary I convinced her to get the magazine for me out of her mom's room and everything she said turned out to be true—only worse. They had a funeral where everybody could see the body (open casket, they call it) and his face was all smashed in so you couldn't even recognize him. He had a bullet hole through his head. They tied a heavy piece of steel (a fan off a cottin gin) around him so he wouldn't float up and they threw him in the river. According to the magazine, they kept beating him with guns, trying to make him cow down to them, but

81

he wouldn't do it. He kept saying that he was just as good as they were and that he'd had lots of white girlfriends up North.

After the trial was over and they knew they'd gotten away with it, they even did an interview where they admitted everything they'd done to him and how Emmett had stood up to them even as he was being killed. When I asked my mother if she'd heard about it, it turned out that she already knew all about it, but never told me because she thought it would upset me too much.

I also found out that they did a survey down South to see what people thought of it, and most people figured that Emmett got what was coming to him. That's probably what made me do what I did next— how brave Emmett Till was—and me just hiding in the dark waiting for Mary to come outside or having Dickie pick her up for me, or trying to leave my place at the exact right moment on the way to school so I'd be going by her place just as she came down the steps— so I'd get to walk with her. Anyway, I thought it would be the best thing to just walk right up the Bakers's front steps, knock on the door and tell Mr. Baker I wanted to talk to him about Mary.

So there I was the next morning, standing out on the road in front of the Bakers'. It was really pouring rain and I was getting soaked, trying to get up the nerve to go up and knock on the door. Dickie came by on his bike and said, "What are you doing standing around out here, Bill? You're not really going to *call* on Mary, are you?"

"Aw go on, Dickie," I said, trying to sound brave. "Mind your own business."

"When a friend of mine commits suicide, that *is* my own business," he said.

I was going to tell him to beat it again but just then Jimmy came out on the porch and saw us standing there.

"Mar—y, Billy Robinson's here," he yelled back into the house.

Dickie took off up the street on his bike, saying that if I wasn't at school by lunchtime he'd send the police after me. Very funny! I couldn't just take off because Jimmy had seen me hanging around, so I went right up and knocked on the door. Mr. Baker opened the door and glared at me.

"Uh...hi, Mr. Baker. Is Mary home?" I was trying to seem confident.

"Mary's *never* home to you, Billy," he said. "And stay away from her! You understand?"

"Well...I..."

Before I could say anything, he slammed the door.

I walked up the road a ways and waited for Mary to come out on her way to school, but her dad drove her. I didn't go to school that day. Even in the rain it

83

was better sitting down at the creek than facing all those kids and teachers with so much on my mind.

About eleven o'clock it stopped raining and the sun came out. I just walked around feeling like an idiot. It was probably just as well that I didn't get to say anything before Mr. Baker slammed the door in my face. I didn't know what I was going to say to him anyway. But when he said Mary wasn't *ever* home to me I should have kicked him in the nuts or something. The rotten bastard! Even worse was not knowing how Mary was feeling about everything. I mean...she kind of didn't even want me to say anything bad about her dad. How was I supposed to ever stand up to him without saying anything bad? He was just going to always insult me if I tried to talk to him. I knew *that*.

I really wanted to talk to somebody about it, but there wasn't anybody. It was like being all tied up in knots. And the funny thing was that I'd almost forgotten about the biggest problem—Mary being pregnant. It was like she'd forgotten about it, too. The last couple of times I'd seen her neither of us even mentioned it—which was very strange. It was as though it was more important to straighten out something with her dad. The next day I rode my bike to school and I didn't even look at Mary's house when

84

I went by. Mr. Higgins was trying to organize his big social studies project. He'd lined up even more students to do a report on their ancestors. I decided that I wasn't having any part of *that* bullshit. When he mentioned it to me again I told him that I didn't see why people had to keep reminding me that I was coloured. All I got for that was another one of his clueless looks. That same week the grade nines were taking counselling on careers and a bunch of aptitude tests to find out what we were supposed to be when we got out of school. I sure wasn't thinking that far ahead. If I couldn't figure out something about Mary, I wouldn't have to worry about my future.

So anyway, there I am sitting in the counsellor's office—Mrs. Bradley—and she's asking me questions about things I like to do and filling out a form. Then she got to a part about how many bedrooms we had in our house and where did everybody sleep—stuff that was none of her business. I just stood up all of a sudden and walked out. On the road the rainwater was running in little shiny streams in the mud, but I hardly noticed anything else because I was pretty mad. When I got to the Bakers' farm I just kept on running right up the path worn into the mud by all those white cows. Boy, was I ever lucky that Mr. Baker wasn't home because he would have been really mad to see me standing there on his back porch like that.

When Mrs. Baker saw me through the kitchen window, she actually smiled at me and opened the door and invited me in—like she wasn't even all that surprised to see me.

Then I was standing in the kitchen, still kind of puffing from running so fast and Mrs. Baker was just looking at me.

"I'd like to talk to you about Mary," I finally said. "If you're not too busy."

She seemed a bit nervous and lit a cigarette, then told me to come into the living room and sit down. Did I ever feel funny sitting in there with Mr. Baker's wife like that.

"You know, Billy, Mary talks about you all the time," she said, sitting down at the other end of the couch and taking a really big puff.

"She does? I didn't know that."

"She says you're the fastest runner in the school."

"I used to be I guess...at Bose Road."

"Well, you get a lot of practice. I see you running up and down the road and through the fields all the time."

That really made me blush. "Uh...I guess you're wondering how come I came over here, eh."

"Something about Mary, Billy?"

"Yeah, I guess so. Mr. Baker sure doesn't want me to see her very much, does he?"

"Well, to be perfectly honest with you, Billy, no he

86

doesn't, and if you think it's because of your colour you're right."

I felt all nervous again. I'd never really discussed this thing with anybody except Mom and Sarah and Dickie, and I couldn't think of anything to say.

"Well, I guess I'd better get going now, Mrs. Baker." I stood up to leave.

"Billy, I'd like you to know one thing. As far as I'm concerned you're as nice a boy as any for Mary to be friends with. I don't care what colour you are, but I'm afraid that as long as Mary lives in this house she'll have to abide by her father's wishes."

I got up and headed for the back door without being able to think of anything to answer back to her. "Thanks a lot anyway, Mrs. Baker," I managed, as I opened the door to leave.

"Listen, Billy, I know it seems like a long time, but in a few years if you and Mary still want to be together, there won't be anything anyone will be able to do about it."

I was halfway down the stairs when she said that and I guess I just stood there and looked up at her for a few seconds.

"Well, thanks again," I said stupidly.

It was raining on the path towards home and I stepped along quickly in the mud, really noticing how beautiful everything was. Beads of water were glistening on the barbed wire fencing like shiny diamonds. I was thinking about what Mrs. Baker had said about me and Mary being together someday. That's probably what made things seem pretty again.

Of course, I still hadn't said anything to anyone about Mary being pregnant.

Chapter 13

"You haven't been studying at all, Billy, and you know it, so don't argue with me."

"I don't need to study all that much, Mom. I always get good marks. Pass the bread, please."

"You just wait 'til you get your first report card," said Sarah. "It's not so easy to do nothing in *high* school and still get good marks."

"Billy's in love, anyway," said Mom. "He's got no time to study."

"Aw, gee whiz, Mom," I said.

"You've been moping around here like a lovesick puppy ever since you met that girl. Keep it up and you're going to flunk right out of school."

"No, I won't. You can't flunk out of grade nine."

Mom asked, "What's bothering you so much that you can't even sleep?"

Which I didn't want to talk about, because I'd been feeling good about going to see Mrs. Baker and this was kind of ruining it.

"Billy, are you listening to me?"

I was poking my fork around in my food.

"Well, what are you so upset about?" Her voice had gotten softer, like she was trying to be nice.

"He's just mad because Mr. Baker won't let him see Mary anymore, that's all," said Sarah.

"Why don't you just mind your own business," I said to Sarah. Then I got up from the table and accidently spilled a big pot of beans on the table which dribbled down and got all over Sarah's dress.

"You stupid little nigger," she yelled.

"Will you stop calling me that!" I yelled right back. "Why do you have to call me that all the time?"

"What a big baby you're turning out to be. Why don't you just take off down to the creek and pout? That's all you do anyway."

I slammed the back door and sat out on the porch, listening to Mom and Sarah talk about me— although I couldn't really make out what they were saying. Then I *really* started missing Mary, but I couldn't even phone her or go over and see her. She'd probably be finishing supper right about then, but we hadn't been able to make any plans to meet that night. All I could do was walk over to her place and sit down in the dark behind the barn to see if maybe she'd come outside.

Then Mom opened the door and asked me to come back inside. Her voice was really gentle as if she and Sarah had decided not to hurt my feelings anymore. I stepped back into the kitchen and Sarah was sitting there smiling at me. Then she actually got up and gave me a big hug.

Mom said, "Okay, Sarah, go ahead. Tell Billy you're sorry."

Sarah hugged me again and gave me a kiss on the cheek. "I'm sorry," she said. "I didn't mean anything." Which, for some reason, made me cry. She hugged me again for probably half a minute and I could see that she really meant it—which brought on even more tears.

"Don't cry, Billy," said Mom putting her arms around me. "We know what you've been going through."

I cried even more, then—like it was all locked up inside of me or something. Sarah gave me her handkerchief and I blew my nose. I felt better but at the same time ashamed for letting them see how upset I was. "I think I'll go lie down a while," I finally said, drying my eyes on Sarah's handkerchief.

"Okay, Bill, you go lie down. And Sarah won't be calling you nigger anymore, either."

I couldn't say anything. I just went into my room

and lied down on the bed, still wiping my face. In a while I climbed out of the window and headed for the Bakers'.

It was really dark and wet, sitting down behind the Bakers' barn. Some kind of little animal was in the bush behind me and I was a bit scared thinking it was a weasel or something like that—or maybe one of the mink that had escaped from that farm on Harris road. After I'd been out there for quite a while somebody opened the Bakers' back door and threw Jimmy's little dog out.

Of course he had to go and start barking and running down towards the barn. I thought maybe Mary would come out, thinking it was me making Jimmy's dog carry on like that. But I was wrong about that, because Mr. Baker followed him out into the yard carrying that old single-shot Cooey he's always shooting rats in the barn with. My heart started pumping real fast when I saw him coming down the path towards me.

"Attaboy, Boots, you scare 'em up and I'll finish him off," he said. Then he started running, following Boots' yelps in the cow pasture. Boy, was I ever getting scared! I couldn't do anything, though, because if I started to run, Boots would come after me for sure. So I just lay down flat behind a log and prayed like I never prayed before that something would save me from getting shot by Mr. Baker.

"You go find 'em, boy. Attaboy, Boots," said Mr. Baker, and pretty soon Boots ran right over to me and started growling and jumping at me. Then the back door flew open and Mary came running and screaming down the path towards her dad. "Daddy, Daddy, don't shoot," she yelled. "It's Billy out there. You're going to shoot him. Daddy, please don't shoot."

I started to breathe easy again, thinking I was saved.

"You go on back in the house, Mary," Mr. Baker shouted after her. "There's nothing out there but a weasel and I'm gonna get him sure as hell. Go back in the house."

I started to get up and tell Mr. Baker it was me but then something told me not to so I just buried my face in the dirt again, and prayed.

Wow! I get shivers even thinking about it now. When Mr. Baker fired I felt the log jump and for a second I thought I was hit. But the blast just tore off a big chunk of wood and missed me clean. Was I ever glad! Then I could hear Mr. Baker reloading his gun so he could take another shot. That's when I started yelling at him not to shoot again, that it wasn't any weasel, but me, Billy Robinson, and I was just going for a walk. He must have known it was me for sure then, but he still didn't say anything. In fact, I didn't hear anything until Mary screamed at her mother who was coming down the path yelling at Mr. Baker to put down the gun.

When I peeked out from behind the log there was a light shining on Mr. Baker and he was just standing there with the gun aimed right at me. Then he lowered it when Mrs. Baker screamed at him. The light from the flashlight was shining in my eyes and I tried to get up but instead I just vomited all over myself and even a bit on Mary when she came down to put her arms around me. And she was in her pajamas, too—like she was ready to go to bed. I guess I could have waited out there all night if Mr. Baker hadn't decided to go hunting. I don't remember much of what happened that night after Mr. Baker stopped shooting and drove away in his car. Mary and her mother were sure upset, though. They were both crying like it was them getting shot at. But anyway, they kind of helped me into the house. Mrs. Baker wanted to call a doctor for me and she kept asking if I was all right.

Mary had her arms around me just about the whole time, too. Mrs. Baker hardly even seemed to be worried about *that*. She must have asked me fifty times if I was sure Mr. Baker heard me call out that it was me hiding in the bush. Boy, that sure seemed like a funny thing for her to say because *she* heard me and she was even further away from me than Mr. Baker. I suppose that would have been a good time for me and

Mary to tell Mrs. Baker that Mary was pregnant, but I don't think either of us even thought about it. When I was feeling okay again I walked on home by myself.

The next morning I was dreaming this really weird dream. There was a DC-3 in the sky, circling over the Bakers' field, (which had been converted from a hayfield into a cornfield). Suddenly it swooped down like a big silver hawk and chased me through the rows of corn until I was out of breath and not able to run anymore. Then it hovered above me and the doors opened and a soldier started pointing some kind of gun at me. Right then Mary, wearing her yellow dress with the Bavarian sash, came walking through the cornfield smiling like everything was going to be okay and reached her hand out to me like she was going to rescue me. Just as I was about to take her hand I heard rap, rap, rap. It was Mom knocking on my bedroom door.

"Shise and rine," she said. "Time to get ready for school." She was shaking my arm, which is what woke me up. (Mom used to always say "shise and rine" instead of "rise and shine.")

"Holy Murphy," I said. "I was having the weirdest dream."

"Where'd you go last night, Billy?" she asked. "Now

don't go telling any tales, because I know you snuck out the window."

"I was just over at Dickie's playing Monopoly's all, Mom."

"From now on no more sneaking out that window. If you do it again I'm gonna nail it shut."

"Okay, Mom."

"Well, at least you weren't out running around with Mary Baker, anyway."

"How'd you know that?"

"She phoned you last night—that's why I came in here and checked on you. Where were you?"

"Just down Bose Road—me and a couple guys were just hanging around."

"What guys?"

"Just Danny and Brian Sutherland."

"Where'd you go?"

"Just *around*—down to Newton."

"You weren't playing knocky, knocky nine doors were you?"

"Nah, we don't do that anymore."

"You better not be. Now come on, Bill. You've got to get ready or you're gonna be late."

"Be right there, Mom," I said, then laid back down for a few minutes trying to see if I could remember any more about the dream. That sure was a strange thing. Mr. Baker could have killed me with his gun and yet nothing had changed between him and Mary and I. One thing though: I was a bit happier, in spite of almost getting shot. At least I knew that Mary loved me, and Mrs. Baker wasn't dead set against me going out with Mary.

Dickie came over after school and we just hung around a fort we had built back in the bush when we were kids. When I told him all about what happened, for once in his life he didn't think everything was so funny.

"Boy, if I was you I'd call the RCMP, Bill," he said. "If Mary's mother hadn't a shone that flashlight on him he coulda shot you, you know."

"Yeah, I guess he could have all right."

"You gonna just let him get away with it?"

"I don't know. What am I supposed to do about it?"

"You should talk to somebody who knows."

"Like who?"

"I dunno. How about Mr. Wesley. He teaches law. He oughta know."

"Yeah … maybe. I already been talking to teachers, though. They don't seem to know nothing."

"Marabelle says Mary should be going to the doctor for regular checkups … so she doesn't get sick or anything."

"I guess you think I don't know that, eh."

"She must be around six or seven weeks gone by now, isn't she?"

"Yeah, I guess so."

"She's gonna start showing pretty soon, you know. Marabelle said if you and Mary don't tell somebody pretty soon, *she's* going to."

"Really, eh. Who's she gonna tell?"

"She's not sure, but she says you can get real sick when you're pregnant if you don't go to the doctor all the time."

"How does *she* know?"

"I dunno."

"Well, she better not tell Mr. Baker. He'll go crazy."

"Yeah, I know. Maybe you and Mary should tell yourselves."

"Tell who?"

"I dunno. How about the nurse? She should know what to do."

Chapter 14

Mrs. Atchison, the nurse, hardly seemed to be listening to me until I said "pregnant." Then her eyes nearly popped out of her head.

"Mary Baker's what? Did you say pregnant?"

"Yup."

She got up from behind her desk and started playing with a ruler. Then her smile came back—the one she had before when she wasn't really listening.

"Has she been to a doctor?" she asked.

"Not yet."

"Oh, so I guess she missed a period, eh Bill?"

"Yeah, I guess so."

"How long ago was this?"

"Almost three weeks ago, now."

"And when did you and Mary make love?"

"I dunno exactly—a few weeks before *that*...I guess...we only did it that one time, though."

"I guess you didn't use anything, eh."

"Nope," I said.

"I would have thought Mary would be the one coming in here telling me about it, instead of you, Bill. How did *that* happen?"

"Well...I dunno...she wants to tell her mom, but somehow she never gets around to it."

"Oh, I see. Do you get along with her parents, Bill?"

"I used to when we were small, but not any more."

"Why's that?"

"Because I'm coloured."

"Oh, I see," she said. Which made me get the craziest thought—like she would say: "Weren't you coloured when you were small?" But of course she didn't say that.

"That must be hurtful, eh Bill," she said, trying to smile. "That's the way it is sometimes."

"I know," I said.

"Well, anyway, Bill..." While she was saying this she went around her desk and started going through some cards in a filing cabinet.

"Let's see...Mary Baker, Abercrombie, Atkins, Baker. Here she is. She's fourteen, eh?"

"Yup, almost fifteen."

"You know, Bill, lots of girls miss their periods. That doesn't necessarily mean they're pregnant. Tell Mary to come see me and we'll find a doctor for her to

100

go see so he can find out for sure. And don't worry, this will just be between the three of us until we find out either way."

Mrs. Atchison was sure being good about every-thing. No lecture, or anything! It was kind of nice to have this thing off my chest. And I was wondering what Mary would say when she found out that I'd told. When the bell rang for the end of the day, she was out on the steps waiting for me, so I guess Mrs. Atchison must have called her in right away.

"You told, eh," she said when I walked up to her.

"Yeah."

"I gotta go to a doctor."

"I know."

The other kids were walking down the steps around us so I took her hand and started going down the steps. People were still staring at us from passing cars, (as usual) but it didn't seem to matter so much.

"Mrs. Atchison is sure nice, eh Bill."

"Yeah, I guess so."

"She's not even going to tell anybody until she finds out from the doctor."

"I know," I said, kicking rocks on the road.

Just then a police car pulled up beside us and a policeman was smiling at us from inside.

"I'm Sergeant Milner. Are you Billy Robinson?" he asked, reaching back and unlocking the back door.

"Yessir," I answered.

"And are you Mary Baker?"

Mary nodded.

"Would you two please come and sit in the back seat for a few minutes? I'd like to talk to both of you."

We went ahead and did what he said. Then he drove down the road and pulled off to the side.

"Is something wrong, sir?" I said, kind of stuttering.

"Well, first of all I'd like to say that you two are not in any kind of trouble with the police so you don't have to worry about that. I'd just like to talk to you for a minute, then I'll drive you home or you can walk home if you prefer that."

"Yessir," I said.

"Bill," he said, opening a notebook, "were you involved in some kind of shooting incident last week?"

"Yessir."

"Uh...that was on the twenty-first of September, eh?" He was writing all of this down in the notebook. "And Mr. Baker, Mary's dad, was involved in the same incident?"

"Yessir, he was."

"Was he shooting at you, Bill?"

"I'm not positive, sir."

Mary was holding my hand really tight, like she was scared.

"Okay, Bill, that's all I wanted to find out right now. Were you there when it happened, Mary?"

"Yes, I was," said Mary in the weakest little voice I'd ever heard her use.

"Well, at this point I'd better tell you, Bill, that your mother has brought a charge against Mr. Baker of trying to shoot you."

"Oh," said Mary.

Then a voice came over the radio and the policeman answered it.

"Maybe we shouldn't say anything," Mary whispered to me.

"I don't know," I answered.

The policeman said: "The boy has just confirmed Mr. Hoffman's statement."

"Did you say Mr. Hoffman?" I asked, really confused.

"Yes, Bill. Mr. Hoffman is actually the one who called us in. Then we contacted your mother and she laid the charge this morning."

"I didn't know Mr. Hoffman knew anything about it," I said.

"Well, apparently he came out to his fence when he heard some screaming and was standing there when everything happened. But we really shouldn't be too interested in that at this point. What I'm going to do is give Mary a ride home and then you and I can have more of a talk about exactly what happened."

"Can I walk home?" asked Mary.

"Oh sure, Miss. That's fine, if you'd prefer. My partner's over at your place now, talking to your mother."

Mary gave me a little hug, then opened the door and stepped out.

"Now, Bill, could you start at the beginning and tell me everything you know about the shooting?"

I told him the whole thing, all right...except about Mary being pregnant and why her dad hated me so much. When I was finished, and he'd taken a bunch of notes, I finally stepped out of the car and headed home. As I walked into our yard I could see Mom looking out the front window at me. She looked really upset. Then she came running down the lawn towards me.

"You should have told me, Billy," she cried, giving me a really big hug. Sarah was even really glad to see me, like I'd been gone on a holiday, or something. She put her arms around me too, and gave me a kiss on the cheek. Mom explained how Mr. Hoffman had heard some noise from his kitchen window and rushed over to where he could get a glimpse of what was happening. He heard me yelling for Mr. Baker not to shoot me and he even saw Mr. Baker with the gun when Mrs. Baker shone the light on him.

They arrested Mr. Baker that night, but he didn't have to go to jail or anything, though, because he was out on bail by eight o'clock. The funny thing about Mr. Hoffman was why he waited so long before reporting it to the police. When I asked Mom that, she asked me how come me and Mary never told anybody. I didn't have an answer for that.

The next day Sarah and I both stayed home from school and went down to the creek to watch the minnows. Dickie and I used to catch them and call them sardines when we were small. It was really a great day to be playing hooky and it was nice just to go walking and not be upset about everything for a change. I guess having my sister with me made a lot of difference, too. She was being so nice I could hardly believe it. She wanted to talk all about school and what we were going to be when we grew up.

This might sound funny but actually I'd kind of been thinking about being a prisoner when I grew up, if Mr. Baker ever found out about Mary being pregnant. It's strange how things can be in the back of your mind all the time making you act a certain way without you even knowing it. Sarah knew exactly what I meant when I told her about being upset a lot of the time.

"I was afraid a lot myself," she said, walking ahead of me on the trail. "Before you came to school I was the only coloured person in the whole school and just about everybody looked at me funny. Like that one time that girl asked me if I could speak Negro."

"You're kidding," I said, surprised. "*Nobody* ever asked me *that*."

She stopped walking and looked back at me for a second. "Billy," she said. "Did you used to think I was mean for not ever wanting you to come over when I was babysitting for Jimmy?"

"Yeah, I guess I did, all right."

"The reason I was so mean was because I knew Mr. Baker didn't want Mary to have anything to do with you and I thought you'd get in trouble."

"That's okay," I said. I told her that I didn't hold it against her but even now I still don't know exactly why she acted so nasty to me whenever I was over at the Bakers'. When we got to the creek we saw Mary sitting on a log, tossing pebbles into the water. Sarah went home to get the clothes off the line before it started to rain and I went to sit with Mary on the log.

"Hi Bill," she said, without looking up. "I guess they're going to put my dad in jail for a long time, eh."

She sure looked sad. I didn't know what to say to her. The wind was blowing a bit and for a minute we just watched the branches sway in the bushes across the creek.

Chapter 15

I was walking across the school grounds, feeling pretty lonely because Mary wasn't at school, when I spotted the Bakers' Oldsmobile parked in the parking lot.

"Hey Billy, will you come here for a minute?" It was Mrs. Baker calling me from the car. I sure wasn't very enthusiastic about talking to her since that night Mr. Baker shot at me. But there really wasn't anything else to do but go and see what she wanted.

"Hi, Mrs. Baker," I said, walking up to the car. I could already smell her perfume coming through the window.

"Billy, would you mind getting in the car for a few minutes? I'd like to talk to you."

"Okay, Mrs. Baker."

As I climbed into the front seat she started the motor and we began to move out of the parking lot.

"I hope you don't mind spending a few minutes with me, Bill," she said.

"I guess not—as long as I'm home in a little while."

"I thought we might drive down to Unwin Park—that's if you don't mind."

"I guess so," I said.

Mrs. Baker was really dressed up nice, like she was going out somewhere really important.

"Are you going to town?" I asked.

"Oh no. Why do you ask?"

"No reason. You just seem really dressed up," I said, which made her smile.

"Do you like my new dress, Billy?"

Wow! That was a funny kind of question for her to be asking me. "Sure," I said.

She lit a cigarette then said, "We're sure sorry about the shooting accident."

"That's okay," I said.

"George wants you to know that, too."

"Who?"

"Mary's father."

"Oh."

"He never would have taken his gun outside if he thought you might be out there, Billy."

"I don't know, ma'am."

She looked at me really hard when I said that.

"You know what the police are trying to say, Bill? They're trying to say that George was trying to shoot you on purpose. Now isn't that the craziest thing."

I didn't say anything for a few seconds because she seemed to be getting upset.

"Mrs. Baker," I finally said, "I don't really know for positive if Mr. Baker knew I was there or not, but I know one thing for sure."

"What's that?" she asked.

"If he didn't hear me yelling at him after he shot, he must be stone deaf."

She didn't answer *that*. We were coming up to the park and I could see a bunch of the guys from school kicking a soccer ball around.

"Are those your friends, Bill?"

"Some of them," I answered. We pulled up and parked right by the Unwin Road community hall.

"I guess I can't fool you, can I, Bill?" she said, shutting off the motor and turning to me with a real serious look on her face.

"Huh?" I said.

"We both know that George heard you, so there's no use kidding ourselves."

"I really don't know, Mrs. Baker," I answered. "When Mary phoned me, didn't my mother tell her I wasn't home? I used to wait out there sometimes for her to come out. That's how she figured it could be me that the dog was barking at. That's why she phoned me—to see if I was home or not."

"You mean to say you waited out there lots of times—out there in the dark when you didn't even know if Mary was home?"

"Yup...sometimes."

"How long would you wait?"

"Depends. Sometimes probably an hour. Otherwise I'd never get to see her—except at school. I couldn't phone her or knock on the door or ask her out or *anything*."

"That's really sad, Bill," she said. "I'm really sorry."

I didn't say anything because thinking about it was making me upset, too. Mrs. Baker just sat there for a while, looking at the kids on the soccer field and smoking. Then she said, "You know, Bill, sometimes people go on for their whole lives fooling themselves about everything."

"I guess so, Ma'am."

"That's how it was with me and George. You know, a long time ago I was in a situation a lot like you and Mary."

"You mean about people being prejudiced?"

"Uh-huh. I'm from Winnipeg. I probably hadn't ever spoken to a coloured person in my entire life until a family moved in a few houses away from us. I

110

was going out with one of the boys so when it got serious my parents sent me to live with some relatives in Vancouver."

"Really?" I said, kind of shocked. "That must have been awful. I never knew that. Does Mary know about that?"

"No, I never told her."

"What a coincidence, eh," I said. "How old were you?"

"We were a bit older than you guys. I was almost eighteen when I moved out here."

"You mean even when you were eighteen you still couldn't go out with him?"

"Well, I guess I *could* have, but everybody was so against it, we just gave up."

"*Him*, too."

"Yeah, well actually he's the one who stopped writing. Then a couple of years later he got married to somebody else—a coloured girl from Nova Scotia."

"Did Mr. Baker ever find out about it?" I asked.

"Well, not at the time. I didn't meet him for a few years after I got out here, but one day I got home from work and he had all my old photos and letters out on the bed."

"Photos of you and your boyfriend?"

"Yeah, and letters, too—all those love letters he wrote to me before we broke it off."

111

"I guess *that* must have really made a big hit with Mr. Baker, eh?"

"Yeah, I think that was the day all our troubles started."

"Uh...I guess I should get going now," I said, feeling a bit embarrassed to be talking about Mrs. Baker's personal affairs. "I have to go to the store for my mom."

"Billy," she said, reaching out and taking my hand. "I want you to know that I'll be moving into town with Jimmy and Mary, and when I do it will be perfectly fine with me if you and Mary still want to see each other."

"Really?" I said. "You're breaking up with Mr. Baker?"

"Yes. I've been thinking about it for a long time now, but somehow this latest thing has given me the courage to actually go through with it."

"Does Mary know?"

"Not yet," she said. "But I'll be telling her pretty soon. I'd appreciate it if you don't mention anything."

"Oh no, I wouldn't do that...not if you don't want me to."

For a minute there I forgot she was holding my hand until she started squeezing it. Then she leaned forward and kissed me on the cheek. Wow! I was really embarrassed when she did that, so I opened the door and stepped out of the car, waving at her as I started to walk on to the Little League baseball diamond.

"Bye, Mrs. Baker," I said.

She sat there for a long time watching me walk away. It's not a long way home from Unwin Park to our place. There's a shortcut at the back of the field through the woods where you come out near Burchart and Roebuck, which is just a few blocks from home. I walked along real slow, thinking about everything. People are sure confusing! I started to think a lot about Mom and how good she was being to me, and about Sarah and how nice she could act—when she wanted to. I thought of the word, dilemma...and that was what Mrs. Baker was—a dilemma.

Chapter 16

"Guess what?" Mary said.

"What?"

"Whadya think?"

"I dunno, what?"

"I went to see the doctor this morning."

Mary had phoned me up and we were doing our usual silly telephone talk.

"Well...*are* you?" I wanted to know.

"Am I what?"

"You know. Are you?"

"I still don't know for sure yet."

"Oh," I said, disappointed.

Then she whispered into the receiver, "It's too soon to know for sure, but I could be."

"Oh great," I whispered back. I don't know why I was whispering. There was nobody home except me.

"Meet me down at the barn as soon as it's dark," she said real fast. Then she hung up.

Down behind the Bakers' barn I was trying to avoid stepping in cow manure on the path from the creek, which is probably three or four hundred feet away. There was no moon that night and it was pitch black. In fact it was so dark that I almost walked into a cow standing in the middle of the path. When I got up to the barn I looked through the window and I could see a dim light coming from the spot that would have been where the top of the ladder rested against the loft planks. It was coming from the small flashlight that Mary was holding. When I climbed the ladder we went over to our usual spot in front of the open hay doors. Right away Mary was kind of snuggling up to me and I started kissing and caressing her. Then she stretched out beside me and started unbuttoning my shirt. Boy, her hands were really warm.

I guess I was getting pretty excited. When I asked her if she wanted to make love again she didn't say anything, but just kept on hugging me and undoing my clothes. I started undressing her and pulling her really close, but before I got very far somebody shone a flashlight on us.

I'll never forget that as long as I live. Mary screamed and tried to get her clothes buttoned up. I was groping around in the dark for my shirt. The light was moving from her to me real fast like the person holding it was teasing us. Suddenly, whoever it was started climbing back down down the ladder without saying a word and took off out of the barn. Wow! We didn't know *what* to think. Whoever it was was acting very strange!

"Oh, great," Mary said, trying to straighten up her clothes. "Who was that? And why did he take off like that? Do you think it was my dad? Holy Christ. What are we going to do now?"

"I couldn't see anything but the light," I said, just as scared probably, "but I don't think it was your dad. He wouldn't have taken off like that."

"Well, who could it be, then?"

"I dunno."

She was holding on to me and I could feel her trembling. We started groping our way over to the ladder and then climbed down. I slowly pushed open the barn door, worried that whoever it was with the flashlight might be hiding outside, ready to pounce on me or something. When we got outside we couldn't run because it was so dark that we'd have just fallen in the mud. So we were kind of feeling our way along the path that led down to the creek for a few minutes, when suddenly a light flickered from probably a hundred feet or so ahead of us. Not knowing what else to do, we got off the trail and made our way over to a clump of trees to hide and wait for whoever it was to come closer. When the swaying light from the flashlight got closer, we heard the sound of someone sobbing and realized that it was Mary's little brother. What a relief *that* was!

"Jimmy!" Mary yelled out to him.

"You better wait for me, Mary...or I'm telling," Jimmy said, between sobs.

"What are you doing out here in the dark all alone?" Mary wanted to know.

"I had to go some place 'cause Mommy and Daddy are having a really big fight." Then he started to cry even more. "And Mommy said she was leaving daddy and we're going to live in town."

"Who's going to live in town?" asked Mary.

"You and me and mommy—at Aunt Betty's."

For a while Mary didn't say anything but just knelt there with her arms around Jimmy. He sure was a brave little guy. Then he said, "I was trying to find you up in the loft...but I thought you'd be mad at me."

"We're not mad at you, Jimmy," I said. "You just scared us because we didn't know who it was."

"Sorry," he said.

Chapter 17

The next day I stayed home from shool waiting to hear from Mary. Mom was looking at me kind of funny, but she didn't say anything mean, though. I guess she knew I was thinking about Mary. Anyway, about eleven o'clock the phone rang and it was Mary telling me that she'd only be able to see me for a few minutes before they left so I should come over right away.

When I got to their place Mrs. Baker had a whole bunch of stuff piled in the front room. It was sure strange being invited right into the house like that. That was the first time I'd ever visited Mary right inside the house—except when the Bakers were on vacation.

"You can come in to visit us on weekends, Bill," said Mrs. Baker, as she hurried around packing things. In a couple of minutes Mary took my hand and led me outside under the big apple tree that I used to snitch apples from when the Bakers' place was part of Hoffman's orchard.

"I'm pregnant, Bill," she said, turning her face away from me like she always did.

I couldn't think of anything to say so we just hugged until Mrs. Baker called us from the porch. Pretty soon a taxi came to take them to the bus. While Mary was sitting in it, she handed me a little chunk of wood to carry around with me so I would think about her all the time. I didn't need that to remind me of her, but it was nice having it, anyway.

I sure had a lot of time to think about everything after Mrs. Baker took Jimmy and Mary to Vancouver. I guess I was pretty lonely, too, but in a way it was kind of a relief not having to worry about Mr. Baker catching us together. After they left I spent the rest of the day walking around a bunch of the places Mary and I had been together. I sure loved her a lot!

Chapter 18

Mom and Sarah were treating me really nice again. They wanted to take me on a picnic down in Bear Creek Park with them but I wasn't very enthusiastic about having fun without Mary around. Dickie dropped by after school and just hung around, trying to make me feel better. After a while I just wanted to be by myself so I said I wasn't feeling very well. Marabelle phoned me and asked about Mary and I said I didn't know anything.

"How come she didn't even phone me or anything?" she asked.

"I don't know," I said. "I'll let you know when I hear from her." Then I hung up.

I suppose I was being pretty mean to everybody, but I wasn't feeling very happy myself. After supper, which I hardly ate any of, I walked down to the creek, thinking all of these really scary things about maybe not ever seeing Mary again or her not liking me when I did see her. There's an old saying that being away from somebody makes you like them even more, but I sure didn't want to have to depend on *that*. Being able to see Mary every day—in spite of everything— was so nice because I could always just watch her looking at me and right away I could tell if everything was the same between us. For instance, the way she'd turn away from you if you said something really important or how she'd kind of get pissed off if you didn't hold her hand. After she left, there was no way of telling if I was really important to her or not.

Anyway, thinking about all that made me miss her even more. And all the leaves were turning those colours they always turn in the fall, too.

It wasn't the same without somebody to say things about them to. It's really funny how I started to think about so many things we had done together— almost like she was dead or something and I was thinking about how it used to be when she was still alive. That night I had a beautiful dream about making love to her in the loft.

Chapter 19

"Bill, Mr. Willard's calling you."

That was Betty Hatfield talking to me. I'd been sitting in the sun, daydreaming, watching the softball game during lunch hour.

"Yessir," I called back, looking up, trying to see where he was.

"Bill, will you come over here for a minute?" he asked.

I got up and walked over to the grassy area where he was teaching some kids how to throw the discus.

"Hey, Bill," he said, giving the discus to this great big kid named Guy Stefanko, who just happened to be one of the best discus throwers around anywhere.

"Hi, Mr. Willard," I said.

"Bill, I'd like you to watch Guy throw and see if maybe you can learn."

"Yessir."

Then Guy wound up and tossed the discus way across the field.

"Guy, would you go get it and show Bill how it's done? Now Bill, Guy's one of the best discus throwers in BC. If anybody can teach you how it's done, it'll be Guy."

"I don't know, sir. I never threw one before," I said, stepping back, thinking about maybe just taking off across the field.

"Herb Ratner sprained his wrist and I thought maybe we could get you to take his place on the track team, Bill."

"I don't think so, sir. I'm pretty busy these days."

"Well, maybe you could just watch Guy for a while. Okay, Bill?"

"I guess so, sir," I said, feeling pissed right off.

"Good."

Guy came back with the discus.

"Guy, Bill Robinson would like you to give him a few lessons. He's one of our best athletes so it shouldn't be too much trouble."

"Hi, Bill," said Guy, who was standing there, squinting because the sun was in his eyes as he looked at me.

"Okay, you two have a workout. Will you drop around to my office after school, Bill?"

"Okay, sir."

"You hold it like this," said Guy, cupping the discus and twirling around in slow motion. Boy, did I ever get railroaded!

After school I was walking down the hall thinking that this was the way it had always been with teachers. They tell you to do something and you just go on and listen to them like they're god or something. I sure couldn't figure out how come Mr. Willard should think I'd make a good discus thrower. The one thing you had to be to throw a discus is really big so that you'd have a lot of weight behind your throw—and I sure wasn't that. I was tall enough—almost six feet, but I didn't weigh more than a hundred-and-thirty-five pounds.

Compared to me, Guy's a regular giant. In fact, that's the first thing I said to Mr. Willard when I entered his office in the gym.

"I think I'm too small to be a discus thrower, Mr. Willard. Guy's at least two-twenty."

For a second he didn't say anything, just got out some things from his drawer.

"Bill, this is Jesse Owens," he said, handing me a picture. "Have you heard of him?"

"Sounds familiar, but I can't quite remember."

Mr. Willard seemed like he didn't believe me.

"You mean to say you don't know about Jesse Owens? He should be one of your heroes."

"I guess not, sir."

"He was the greatest black athlete of all time. In the 1936 Olympics in Germany, he won so many events that the Nazis had to reconsider what Hitler said about Germans being superior to everybody else."

Then Mr. Willard showed me a picture of Jackie Robinson—which I recognized right away.

"That's Jackie Robinson, sir."

"I thought you'd recognize him, Bill. He was the first coloured man to ever play in major league baseball."

Then Mr. Willard got a real serious look on his face. "You know, Bill, *you* people have a natural ability in athletics—especially in sports that need quick reflexes and speed. That's why I was glad when you and Sarah came to this school—because I figured there'd be a good chance of training you to meet your god-given ability in sports—maybe even to the level of provincial or even national competition."

I started to say something but Mr. Willard was really taken up with what he was saying. "Oh, sure," he continued, "you lost a race a few weeks ago, but that was because you were all upset over the Baker girl. Now, since she's moved away, I hope you can give more attention to our track and field program." Then he sat down and waited for me to say something.

"Mr. Willard, I...I don't think I'm big enough to throw a discus," I said, feeling tears welling up in my eyes.

"I got to get going, sir. My mom's waiting for me."
I turned and ran out of the gym and over across the
playing field where Guy Stefanko was waiting to show
me how to throw the discus.

When I went past the Bakers' place I started to get
really lonely for Mary. Nothing had changed with Mr.
Willard. He still figured I was a football or something.
And then a really funny thing happened. Standing on
the road, looking at the Bakers' farm, it was like I'd
had the same experience before. I mean... like everything was the same as some other time in the past.
It's really hard to explain but I felt like I was in a
dream or something. Then I remembered running up
to the Bakers' back porch and Mrs. Baker asking me
to come in and sit down. I had the weirdest urge to do
it all again.

A car came down the road and I could see that it
was Mr. Baker. I started to walk away real fast, but he
came past his driveway and pulled the car up beside
me. He had a really angry look on his face. For a second
I thought he was going to say something really mean
to me or even try to hit me, but he didn't do anything.
By the time he drove away my heart was pounding fast
like it was going to come right out of my chest.

People say that just before you die your whole life
passes in front of your eyes. Well, that's the way I felt
then. Not that I thought I was going to die, or anything,

but wanting to run away was the story of my life. Maybe I was able to do what I did for that reason—and a lot of other things, like Mr. Willard thinking I was a natural athlete just because I'm coloured. Or it could have just been because I was missing Mary so much. Anyway, when Mr. Baker came back down the road and slowed down beside me again I just stood there staring at him. Then when he started to say something I yelled: "You rotten, prejudiced son of a bitch, why don't you just fuck right off?"

He sure looked stunned when he heard that and he opened his car door to get out, but by then I was already across the ditch, heading for home, thinking that it didn't matter that I was running. At last I'd finally said exactly what I'd been wanting to say to him for years.

Chapter 20

Dickie said that it was pretty dangerous to be swearing at Mr. Baker because he had a lot of pressures on him, and he could just explode and shoot me or something.

"If I were you," he said, "I'd stay clear of him—that's for sure."

We were sitting down by the creek, tossing rocks at a tin can floating in the water.

"I mean..." he continued. "He hasn't got any family left or anything."

"You sound like you feel sorry for him," I said.

"I don't feel sorry for him. It's just kind of dangerous egging him on like that."

"I'm not egging him on."

"Okay, but don't say I didn't warn you."

I got up for no reason at all and walked a couple of steps away. "Hey, Dickie," I said, throwing another rock at the Royal City Foods can, "You want to go to town with me tomorrow?"

"What for?"

"To see Mary," I said, trying to sound casual.

"Nope."

"How come?"

"'Cause."

"'Cause why?"

"'Cause I'm already playing hooky with Marabelle."

"Oh."

"We're going to Redwood Park on a picnic."

"Marabelle could come, too," I said.

"Aw, she wouldn't want to."

"How do *you* know?"

"How are you getting there?" he asked, seeming a little bit interested.

"Pacific Stage."

"Marabelle doesn't like long bus rides. It makes her feel like throwing up."

"I bet. I never heard of *that*."

"Really! It makes her sick. Honest."

"I guess I'll have to go by myself," I said, feeling disappointed in not having somebody along.

"Did you find out if she's pregnant or not?"

"Yup."

"Well, is she?"

"Yeah...looks like it."

"What are you guys going to do about it? She's not going to just get unpregnant, you know."

"I know. Not much I can do. It's all outta my hands now anyway."

The next morning I got dressed and ate breakfast with Mom and Sarah just like I was going to school. Then I ran down to the bus stop at Roebuck and Newton Road and caught the bus for Vancouver. My stomach was kind of churning around like I had butterflies or something. I was thinking about whether I should just be popping up at Mary's aunt's place without them knowing I was coming. I knew Mary'd be glad to see me, anyway. At least I could be sure of that! Watching the scenery go by I got to thinking about the time I was playing murder ball with a bunch of kids in a field at Roebuck and Newton, and I saw my dad go by on the bus. I hadn't seen him for about three years and he just smiled and waved at me, then sat back in his seat like he was thinking about something else. I just took off running then, too—way out in the bush so the other kids couldn't see me. I remember telling Mom about it and she said that he was probably too busy thinking about white women.

The bus pulled into the Vancouver depot on Georgia Street and I got down, feeling pretty confused about how I was going to get to Mary's aunt's place. I had her address, all right—near Hastings and Cassiar—but I didn't have enough money for a taxi and I wasn't too sure how to get a bus over there. Walking in Vancouver is a lot different than walking in Newton. People seem to mostly ignore a person. Going up Georgia I had to really dodge all the pedestrians or I would have got trampled. I was walking up real straight, though, because my Aunt says I have a tendency to shuffle sometimes.

It was my idea to ask somebody what bus I took to get to Cassiar and Hastings, but every time I kind of smiled at somebody to see if they were friendly it seemed like they just ignored me. Then when I came to the end of the block at a red light, a big convertible came up to the curb beside me and stopped.

The guys in it were real big, and they all were wearing the same sweaters—like they were on a sports team or something. They were having a good time laughing at something.

Then I realized that what they were laughing at had something to do with me because one of them pointed at me and they all had a *really* good laugh. I was starting to feel nervous standing there waiting for the red light to change. It's sure not very much fun having people gawk at you like that. When the light finally changed I took off real fast across the street but the car just stayed right beside me as I went through the intersection—which made me worry that those guys were going to do something to me. Then they came right up close to the curb beside me and one of them yelled: "Hey, boy...who owns you?" Then another guy said: "Nigger, nigger, pull the trigger." After that, they took off real fast up the street, burning a patch of rubber, and laughing like it was the funniest thing ever.

That sure made me feel bad. What actually bothered me most was being embarrassed because a few people were staring at me. One guy about my age was even smiling. I didn't want anybody to think I had done something wrong. One old man must have seen what happened because he came over to me and reached his arm out to touch my shoulder. He seemed to be feeling pretty bad about it, too. "Don't pay them no mind, son," he said, in a kind of creaky voice. "They're just young hoodlums."

For a second I was going to say something—and I did appreciate what the old man had said—but I just kind of half smiled, then started walking real fast back down towards the bus depot.

It made me feel a little guilty, not talking to the old man because he was really trying to make me feel better. But it's kind of hard to talk about people just pulling up in a car and yelling insulting things to a perfect stranger.

The sidewalk seemed even more crowded than it did before. All the faces seemed to be staring at me. I remember talking about psychology with Mr. Higgins once and he said that that was called *paranoia*. Anyway, it sure was an unpleasant way to feel. For a while, nothing was important except getting out of the city and away from all of those staring people. I had to wait in the bus depot for a couple of hours, but it was sure a relief to be back on the Pacific Stage, heading home.

Chapter 21

I was asleep when the bus pulled into Newton in front of Jack's General Store. The bus driver came back and woke me up and said for me to hurry up because he had to get going. When I first looked up and saw his face, for a second I thought it was Mr. Baker because I was dreaming about me and him meeting and having it out once and for all.

"I almost took you down to White Rock, son," he said, smiling, then walking back up the aisle.

Well, at least I was home again. It was kind of like coming back from the wars or something. I felt like I'd just been dragged through a knothole. Heading up Newton Road from King George, I was turning everything over in my mind. It's weird how a person can kind of lose track of what's really important. For instance, I'd been thinking about seeing Mary so much but when those guys called me names it didn't seem so important anymore. Not that I didn't love her or anything, but I was feeling like something had happened to me that changed my mind about things. (I guess that sounds pretty mixed up). Anyway, I started to feel pretty calm, like I'd made a very important decision, but I didn't know what I'd made up my mind about. It was just a feeling.

At school the next day there was a note on my locker to see Mr. Willard after school, but I didn't go because I'd decided never to have anything to do with sports as long as I lived.

Dickie was there waiting for me by the bicycle stands, looking like he'd just lost his best friend or something.

"Hi, Bill," he said, unlocking his bike and heading out of the parking lot.

"Hi, Dickie."

"Guess what happened?"

"I don't know. What?"

"I broke up with Marabelle last night."

"Didja?" I said, but it really didn't register on me too much.

"Aw, never mind, Bill. You think nobody's got problems but you." He got on his bike and coasted away, then turned around and gave me a hard, cold stare, like he was pissed off. I sure didn't want Dickie to be mad at me because he was the only friend I had.

136

"Hey, wait up, Dickie," I called after him, sprinting up the road as fast as I could.

Mr. Willard came by in his car and said, "Attaboy, Robinson! Run like that at the track meet and we'll win for sure."

"Up yours!" I yelled, which probably surprised me as much as it surprised him, because, besides what I'd said to Mr. Baker, I don't remember ever saying anything like that to an adult in my entire life. You should have seen the look on his face!

"Hey Dickie," I yelled, "Wait up."

Dickie stopped riding and got down but he didn't turn around to look at me.

"Whadya break up with Marabelle for?" I asked, coming up to him, puffing.

"I dunno," he said. Wow! The guy was almost crying.

"Didn't she say?"

"Albert's got a car—that's why."

"Albert Stasiac? That new kid from Panorama Ridge? You mean she likes *him* better?"

"Looks like it."

"How do you know? I bet she doesn't."

"Have you seen his car?"

"Yeah, big deal."

"They're going to the Surrey Drive-In tonight."

"How do you know?"

"Albert's been bragging all over the place."

Dickie was sure feeling rotten over this. When I saw how broken up he was I couldn't say any of the things that were on my mind—like who'd want a girlfriend who'd ditch a person for a guy with a car, anyway? While we were walking along, Albert's blue '56 Meteor came down Roebuck. Marabelle was sitting next to him, but she just stared straight ahead.

You should have seen the look on Dickie's face when he saw them. People are sure proud sometimes. I think what bugged Dickie the most was losing Marabelle to a shiny car, which probably made him feel kind of worthless.

And seeing Marabelle with Albert might make him cry, so I walked a bit faster so I wouldn't be able to see his face.

"Hey, Bill," he called back, "You wanna go down to the creek?"

"Sure," I said, trying to sound casual, like nothing special was happening.

At night I lay awake for a long time, just looking at the stars out of my bedroom window, thinking about a whole bunch of things...mostly Mary. There were millions of stars and the moon was was really bright, like the night Mary recited that poem out behind the Bakers' barn. That thing with Dickie and Marabelle breaking up was bugging me, too. Albert was like a lot of things in life a person has to watch out for. Like Mr. Baker, for instance—and people trying to make a person feel bad because of what he looks like. In fact, after that night I began to think of a lot of problems that come along as just other Alberts. In the morning I told Sarah about that and she asked: What do you think you are—a philosopher, or something?

Chapter 22

"You'll be a credit to your race, Billy."

That was Mrs. Bowsman, the vice principal, talking. I wasn't hardly paying any attention until she said *that* because I was thinking about maybe talking to Mary on the phone after school.

"And you'll be doing your people a service too, by showing how well-educated and intelligent a Negro can be."

She was talking about me going to university and being a teacher.

"Not only that, but there's very little prejudice among teachers, Bill. You'd be accepted right away." She smiled warmly when she said that and for a second I thought that she was just kidding, but then it occurred to me that she was smiling out of pride.

"Oh, I know you probably can't wait to get out of

school so you can go and help your people in Mississippi or somewhere, but you know there's even a greater opportunity right here."

"Is there, ma'am?" I asked, trying to sound a bit sarcastic.

"Well, Bill, as a teacher you'll be reaching a lot of young people who otherwise wouldn't have had the opportunity to know a member of your race. You'd be contributing just as much to the cause right here at home as you would getting yourself beaten up in a freedom march."

"I guess so," I said. I remember thinking: That sounds like a funny thing for her to be saying because I'd never even considered going in a freedom march. In fact, I wasn't absolutely sure what a freedom march was.

The bell rang which meant that noon hour was over.

"Well, Bill," continued Mrs. Bowsman, still smiling warmly, "I'm glad we got a chance to have this little chat. I hope you'll give it some serious thought."

"Oh, I already thought about it lots of times, ma'am," I said. "But I don't think I want to be a teacher, though."

"Why not, Bill?" She sounded really surprised.

"Because teachers don't make much money, ma'am." I started walking out of the room, thinking that the whole noon hour was down the drain, talking about what I should be when I grew up. Then I turned around to look at Mrs. Bowsman. She smiled back warmly, but not half as warmly as she had been smiling.

Believe it or not, I was actually kind of waiting for Mary to come out and take my hand like she used to. I'd been daydreaming about her all day, wondering how she was doing at her aunt's place. It's pretty hard to explain, but sometimes if you don't have somebody near who you love, you can kind of pretend like they're with you anyway, thinking about all the things you're thinking about and experiencing all the things you're experiencing. I think it's called "schizophrenia" if you start talking to them, though.

Taking a shortcut across a field, I got to thinking about Mrs. Bowsman taking a special interest in me. Especially what she said about me being a credit to my race. I'd heard that before on television. This announcer guy was talking to an Indian who was a movie star and he said that the guy was a credit to his race.

Then I got to wondering if people would say that Dickie was a credit to *his* race if he did something really special—like invent something maybe. But all this philosophy stuff soon passed out of my mind and I lay down in the middle of the field which was full of tall green grass and tons of dandelions. Was the sky ever blue! For a while I was really feeling calm (for a change), not even thinking about how things were going to work out, just watching some clouds drifting across the sky and wondering why everybody couldn't have just left me and Mary alone.

Chapter 23

Subpoena To A Witness

Canada Regina vs. Baker

Province of British Columbia Columbia, County of Westminster, District of Surrey

To: William J. Robinson of 6635-Roebuck Rd.

Surrey BC

Whereas George Robert Baker has been charged that he, the accused, on the 18th day of September A.D. 1959, at the said district of Surrey, in the County of Westminster, did commit the felony of assault with a deadly weapon upon the person of William James Robinson.

That's exactly what the blue paper said. The policeman who gave it to me was real nice and everything, but I was really nervous, thinking about being a witness in court.

"There's nothing to it, Bill," he said, getting back into his RCMP car. "All you have to do is tell what happened."

Pretty soon he was zooming up the street and I was wishing he'd have stayed for a while because I had a bunch of questions to ask him. Like, for instance, how come it said "Regina vs. Baker." That's a city in Saskatchewan. I had to talk to somebody about it right away. For a minute I started running real fast towards home, but then I slowed down because I felt funny about showing it to Mom. Not that she wouldn't know what to do or anything, but... well, I guess I hadn't been paying much attention to her and Sarah lately and maybe they were feeling a bit hurt because I was ignoring them so much. Mom was waiting to see me down at the end of our driveway.

"Come on, son," she said, taking my hand as I walked up to her.

"Hi, Mom," I said.

"The policeman found you, eh, Bill?" she said.

"Yeah, he gave me this." I waved the blue paper at her and she took it and read it while we walked up the driveway.

"How come it says 'Regina'?" I asked.

146

"Billy Robinson, don't you even know *that*? That just means that it's the Crown or the government that's charging Mr. Baker with committing a crime—that's all."

"Oh," I said, still confused, but relieved that Mom seemed to know a lot about courts and things.

We walked into the kitchen where Sarah was fixing black-eyed peas (which are really beans). Mom sat down at the table, still looking at the paper, and I stood around for a few minutes, just thinking about how lucky I was to have Mom and Sarah.

"You gonna be home for supper tonight, Bill?" Sarah asked, lifting the big pot of black-eyed peas on to the stove.

"Yup," I said.

"Good, 'cause we're having something special." She was kind of smiling slyly, like she knew something that I didn't.

"What's so funny, sissy?" I asked.

Then she really started laughing and giggling. "Is my brother ever dumb," she said. "Do you mean to stand there and tell me you don't know what day it is today?"

Then I thought: Holy Christ—it's my birthday!

Mom folded up the paper and came over to give me a hug. "Happy Birthday," she said, a little bit sad. "You sure must have had a lot of things on your mind to forget your own birthday."

It was almost like a real family reunion. Sarah made all the special things I like to eat and Mom told stories about when she was a girl in Wildwood, Alberta. I really laughed when she told us that she was scared she was pregnant after the first time she kissed a boy. I sure knew better than that.

The next day I went to school crossing my fingers that I'd get a letter from Mary. At recess I took off and waited down the road from our house for the mailman. It was almost like a miracle. When the mailman saw me on the side of the road, he stopped his jeep and handed me a letter and it was from Mary. I was so glad I guess I forgot to thank him, just started walking down the trail towards the creek. That was sure a funny feeling. I was actually kind of scared to open it.

A little rabbit was looking right at me up ahead on the trail, almost like he knew something important was happening. A woodpecker started banging away up in some tree. I read the return address over again. It was for me, all right. I began thinking about all the things me and Mary had done together since we were little kids. I remembered that time when I was about six years old and the Bakers had taken me and Mary to the Stanley Park zoo. What I remembered most was Mr. Baker laughing at me and Mary holding hands, and teasing me about being Mary's boyfriend. He was really nice to me then.

Anyway, I finally opened the letter when I got to the creek and started reading real fast.

Dear Bill,

It's really nice in here, but I miss everything in the country. Maybe you can come visit us sometimes. I'll be going to Templeton starting next Monday. It's a really big school and a lot of the kids have their own cars. The basketball team is really good, too. I was there yesterday signing in and already met some of the kids. I think I'm going to like it a lot. Mom said we probably won't be going out to our place for a long time because she's getting divorced from Dad. You know that problem that I have? Well, I won't have it for long because my aunt knows a special doctor who is going to be able to help. Well, I better say goodbye because a friend of mine is coming up the steps.

Love, Mary Baker.

There are probably all kinds of words to describe how I felt after reading that letter, but all I can think of is that I was really sad. I guess the first thing I did was take that chunk of wood out of my pocket and toss it into the creek. Then I sat there and watched it sail away with the other twigs and leaves that had fallen from the trees. At least it floated!

I guess that's all there is to tell. Oh, the trial was

pretty scary and everything, but I didn't have to do very much—only tell the judge that Mr. Baker might have been shooting at me that night. What really fixed him, though, was Mr. Hoffman telling all that he'd seen from his place. Mom said that she didn't think a five-hundred-dollar fine was very much punishment for him. But I think he lost a lot more than that. He lost Mrs. Baker and Jimmy and Mary—same as me.

The End.

Interview with the Author

Question: *What has Truman Green been doing since publishing* A Credit To Your Race *in 1973?*

Truman Green: After I graduated from UBC in 1968 I got a job as an English Marker for the Surrey School Board, a position I held for two years. Throughout the seventies I worked as a carpenter, foreman, and site supervisor in the construction industry. Until I retired a couple of years ago, I had a small business as a home renovations contractor. I'm still single and now live within a couple miles of the Roebuck Road acreage where we lived in the 1950s.

Q: *How many publishers did you send the manuscript of* A Credit To Your Race *to? Were there any personal responses? Any old rejection letters stashed at the back of your socks drawer?*

TG: I would guess about twenty-five since 1973. Of all these submissions only two responses can be considered even remotely encouraging—one from Dennis Lee of Anansi Press, who let me know that the book was "probably" publishable, but didn't go on to explain exactly why he wouldn't publish it.

About 1975 I got the bright idea to send it to the CBC and received a note claiming that while the sentiments and ideas expressed in the book were admirable, they didn't know exactly how they would go about externalizing Billy's thoughts in a way that would make it workable as a television drama. I was so encouraged by this near-acceptance that I wrote them back again, asking that they reconsider. This time they advised me that they didn't know of an actor who would be suitable to play the role of Billy Robinson.

A CREDIT TO YOUR RACE

Q: *I find it interesting that there are no explanatory notes in the original edition of* A Credit To Your Race. *Most self-published book covers are busy with information. But your cover gives no author's biography or story synopsis. Only that enchantingly intricate pen-and-ink drawing of a young man in idyllic repose. Why did you decide to self-publish?*

TG: When the publisher asked me to do an interview to go along with this re-release of my novel I probably agreed because it presented an opportunity for me to provide some information about the book and the creation of the first edition, although on reflection I realized interviews of this sort are usually reserved for famous writers so I'm a bit concerned that this interview idea might be somewhat presumptuous—particularly as the book has probably not been read by more than two-hundred people or so.

Regarding the absence of explanatory notes in the original edition, somewhere along the line I developed the notion that novels should stand on their own without interference, in a similar fashion that paintings in an art gallery shouldn't come with a recording of the artists' statements or critics' critiques blaring in the background as viewers go through the gallery. I see all novels as pieces of artwork that should succeed or fail only with regard to how the reader responds to the work, without being supplied with laudatory hints from introduction writers or anyone besides the author, whose bias will always be assumed by the reader.

After the initial rejection slips from the big publishers like McClelland & Stewart and Douglas & McIntyre, I was still convinced that I had written a unique little story that was at least as interesting as a lot of the fiction that was being published in Canada at the time. (Ed.: 1973 was the publication year of *The Book of Eve* by Constance Beresford-

Howe, *The Temptations of Big Bear* by Rudy Wiebe, *Rat Jelly* by Michael Ondaatje, and *Canada and the Canadians* by George Woodcock. *That's Me in the Middle* by Donald Jack was the top Canadian seller.)

The drawing of Billy on the cover of the original edition was done by Phyllis Greenwood, a Vancouver artist who, at the time, was my very close friend. Phyllis brought the story to the attention of her friend, Reg Rygus, who had obtained a federal grant under a program called Opportunities for Youth to begin a small publishing venture which he called Simple Thoughts Press. All of the physical work of typing, printing, binding, and collating was done by Phyllis, Reg, and his brother Ron Rygus, as well as Phyllis' twin girls, Alexis and Aleteia, who were eight years old at the time.

The costs of publishing were met by the government grant administered by Reg Rygus and by the voluntary assistance of my friends. I wasn't out of pocket a single penny, but without more than a little help from my friends—particularly Phyllis Greenwood—the so-called "self"-published edition would have never happened. In fact it's not really true that the book was "self-published," which implies that the author took on and completed the many tasks of publishing, as I really had very little to do with the publishing effort, besides helping to collate the pages in a short session at a space that had been rented by Reg Rygus for his publishing venture.

Q: *How did you publicize and try to distribute your novel?*

TG: We didn't have any resources for publicizing the book, and distribution was limited to me going around to a few bookstores and asking to see the managers. I remember when Duthie Books was still on Robson Street I went down there and Bill Duthie was at the counter. I told him that I'd written this little novel and he quickly glanced through a copy then told me he'd take forty of them for his store. Of course, not knowing Bill Duthie's helpfulness with new writers, I assumed that he was making a business decision to buy these copies, and besides selling three copies to Woodwards Stores, and perhaps twenty at an arts and craft sale in Ladner, these sales represented all of our successful distributing efforts. The rest of the three hundred copies we had produced went to friends and acquaintances, most often for free. I think that initially I kept three or four copies for myself, but after years of handling them, by 2000 or so, all I had left was about three hundred unbound pages. About six years ago my friend, Val Barker, bought a fairly pristine copy from an online bookseller for fifty dollars and gave it to me as a gift. I've since discovered that a few American universities have copies in their libraries. The original edition seems to have become a bit of a collector's item.

Q: *How did it feel when Anvil Press contacted you about republishing* A Credit To Your Race *nearly forty years since the first edition?*

TG: I first became aware that my book was on a shortlist of books for possible re-publishing when reading the blog of Vancouver's Poet Laureate, Brad Cran. I think he had posted a list of thirty or so Vancouver-area books and had asked the question: "Which of these books would you like to see republished?" and had invited readers to respond. Being fairly used to having my book rejected, my response was something like "nice, but of course my book will never come in close to winning."

Within a few months I received phone calls from Brad Cran, Wayde Compton, and Brian Kaufman, each of them telling me that *A Credit To Your Race* had been chosen for

154

the Legacy Books Project and would be republished. So, yes that was very good news for me.

Q: *Why have you added a few-hundred-words-long introductory chapter for this republication of your novel? You let the rest of your novel stand on its original text. Why add those few new words to the beginning? As I read them I think your revision sets the stage for Billy Robinson's life nicely. Now his mother's employment is explained, something that was inexplicably left out of the original version, and the "divorce" word is said out loud in the revision, which was only implied in the novel by Billy's father's absence which was often observed but never explained. But are there more reasons than only clarity for your brief revisions?*

TG: The edition Anvil Press is publishing is basically the original edition with a new first chapter, along with some very minor revisions in the rest of the story that I considered appropriate. After forty years I had a lot of ideas about how it could be revised. I remembered that one thing that really irked me back in the fifties and sixties was how black people had been portrayed in Hollywood films. As Billy complains in the revised Chapter One, there were very few black people in the movies who weren't portrayed as idiots, fools, or the butt of some white person's racist comments or jokes.

I really enjoy the old Hollywood movies and now that they're available on TCM I spend a lot of time watching them, still very aware of how black people were portrayed then. In fact, I was just watching an old movie the other day in which the black actor known as Stepin Fetchit was going through his usual stupid-Negro routine for the amusement of his fellow characters and the film's audience, so I think it is authentic of me to have included this aspect of Billy's disenchantment in the revised version of the novel, as our

155

family was very much aware at the time that the movies were full of derogatory, insulting, and mocking portrayals of black people. Perhaps only the native peoples of North America, whose lands were confiscated by invaders from Europe, were treated with less respect than blacks in the so-called "Western" genre of Hollywood filmmaking.

Because movies then had such a huge cultural and social impact, I think the Hollywood moguls were in a position to aid in the transition of America from a racist nation, but instead they chose to encourage bigots and reactionaries by portraying blacks as buffoons, idiots, and fools to be made fun of. When I wrote the new first chapter I decided to include some mention of the lack of common decency exhibited by the Hollywood moguls.

Q: *The clarity of the language expressing your protagonist's observations and thoughts and feelings about being the only member of a different race in their entire school and neighbourhood are the most striking part of the novel for me. 1960s Canada was a very racist place before the multicultural branding process began, and "You people" and "He (or she) is a credit to their race" were common everyday Canadian expressions. Billy Robinson paints a very clear picture of what it felt like to live amongst the vapid racism of many of his neighbours and peer group.*

TG: I find it very interesting that you would make this observation regarding Billy's direct explanations to the reader about how he was feeling about the events that were unfolding. In fact, according to my most memorable rejection letter, Billy's personal observations and complaints were the greatest factor in making the novel unpublishable. Here's the entry from that particular letter, the writer of

156

which I'll keep anonymous. It was addressed to a literary agent who forwarded it to me.

"While Truman shows some obvious writing skills, I'm afraid we can't move ahead with this novel. The chief problem is that he constantly tells the reader how he feels without allowing the reader to experience the emotional response to racist behaviour. And at the end of the day he really doesn't have much of a story to tell. The boy-gets-girl-pregnant-in-forbidden-circumstances scenario is far from new. Beyond this very little happens. It seems he is far too preoccupied with getting the message across that the protagonist suffered unreasonable personal pain as opposed to weaving together a story that strikes the reader at a deep level."

So it's quite interesting to me that you appreciated the technique of Billy directly expressing his thoughts, as that publisher implied that this technique was in flagrant contradiction to some cast-in-concrete convention that novelists must be sure that their characters show and not tell. I feel that Billy's thoughts, expressed directly to the reader, are the most interesting and touching parts of the book and I'm happy to know that you agree with me. I remember thinking at the time that perhaps the publisher should reread Anne Frank's diary or *The Catcher in the Rye*, in which the protagonists similarly spend a lot of time complaining to the reader about what was happening to them and how they were being affected emotionally.

Q: *All writers are compelled to write, but not all writers feel compelled to publish, so I'm wondering what you've been writing since* A Credit To Your Race *was published in1973. Are there any other Truman Green novels or short stories stashed in a bottom drawer?*

TG: I've written quite a few short stories, of which only one has been published—"Jason Loves Cory"—which was published in Emily Pohl Weary's magazine *Kiss Machine* in 2005 and reprinted at the online magazine theTyee.ca. "Jason Loves Cory" is a creative non-fiction story about two of my friends who died of drug and alcohol overdoses. I have also had three Science articles published in Australia's *New Dawn Magazine* called "The Placebo Effect," "Antibodies as Determinants of Efficacy in Flu Vaccine Studies," and "Epigenetics," and they are posted on my blog. (Ed.: search "Truman Green's Science Rumours.")

I have written a 3500-word tribute to Jonathan Swift's essay, *A Modest Proposal,* which I titled *Smart Animals,* which can also be read on my blog. *Smart Animals* is about an alien species which sends a giant spacecraft to earth in search of new sources of protein for their boring diet. I really like it and it still makes me laugh out loud every time I read it, but so far I've probably had ten rejection slips from magazine publishers. If you recall, in *A Modest Proposal,* Swift concludes that the Irish, in order to stave off poverty and starvation, should eat the children of the poor. Well, similarly, my alien spacecraft officers, Plaxon and Plasmidian, get into a bit of disagreement about the morality of considering an entire alien species as food.

Q: *It's been nearly forty years since the original three hundred copies of* A Credit to Your Race *were published and, as you observed at the beginning of this interview, probably only about two hundred people have ever read the book. Now that your novel is at last being published by a commercial publisher and will be available in all the Vancouver Public Libraries, what do you anticipate will likely be the most interesting part of this unusual experience?*

158

TG: Well, for most of those forty years I've had this idea that I'd written a story that was unfairly passed over by publishers. In a few months from now, when the reviews and responses start coming in, I'll be finding out if this private little fantasy is correct or if readers are in fact a lot less enthusiastic about the story than I have been.

Either way, there'll be a bit of closure and I'll have to accept the verdict of readers, which, after all, is the only one that really means anything.

About the Author

Truman Green graduated from UBC in 1968 with a BA in English Literature and American History. Recent publication credits include a creative non-fiction story, "Jason Loves Cory," published in *Kiss Machine,* and science-related articles in Australia's *New Dawn Magazine*. Truman lives in Surrey, BC.